MORE PRAISE FOR

A TASTE OF HONEY

"*A Taste of Honey* has the power of memoir and the poetry of fiction. Suddenly, it is 1968 once more, with all of the hope and violence and seismic change that rocked the cities that summer. It's all here and it's all beautifully rendered. This book is a gem."

—Chris Bohjalian, author *Secrets of Eden*

"Jabari Asim has written a brilliant coming-of-age tale filled with compelling characters navigating race relations in 1968, navigating familial and neighborhood demands, and triumphantly reaffirming what it means to be human. A lovely, lyrical collection of connected stories that will leave readers breathless and ecstatic with passion and joy."

—Jewell Parker Rhodes, author of *Yellow Moon*

"Offering the bitter with the sweet, Jabari Asim's first collection of stories, *A Taste of Honey*, serves up a multilayered dish. Asim ranges through and across a Midwestern African American community in the wake of the civil rights movement and the social changes of the last forty years, writing from the inside out and unforgettably bringing to life a world that still is too seldom seen in American fiction."

—John Keene, author of *Annotations*

"Jabari Asim's rich short stories read like a novel . . . full of people we love getting to know—Rose Gabriel, Pristine, Ed, Reuben, and Guts. I particularly loved the male characters in these pages . . . men who live by their brains and their brawn, shelter their children, their community. They embrace their wives. They love hard, laugh deep, and cry inside."

—Denise Nicholas, author of *Freshwater Road*

A Taste
of
Honey

A Taste

of
Honey

Stories

Jabari Asim

Broadway Books
New York

Copyright © 2010 by Jabari Asim

All rights reserved.
Published in the United States by Broadway Books,
an imprint of the Crown Publishing Group,
a division of Random House, Inc., New York.
www.crownpublishing.com

BROADWAY BOOKS and the Broadway Books colophon
are trademarks of Random House, Inc.

Library of Congress Cataloging-in-Publication Data is available
upon request.

ISBN 978-0-7679-1978-4

Printed in the United States of America

Design by Donna Sinisgalli

1 3 5 7 9 10 8 6 4 2

*f*or my wife, Liana,

"to whom I owe the leaping joy"

*t*o Leonidas and A.C.,

with gratitude

Looking back on when I was

a little nappy-headed boy . . .

STEVIE WONDER, "I WISH"

Acknowledgments

Thanks to Janet Hill for getting this project started. Thanks to Christine Pride for seeing it through to the end. Thanks to Joy Harris for prudent counsel. Thanks to my parents for teaching me that family comes first. Thanks to the five geniuses—Joseph, G'Ra, Nia, Jelani, and Gyasi—for being exactly who they are.

Contents

I'd Rather Go Blind   1

Something Like God   12

Zombies   26

The Genius   37

Sic Transit Gloria   52

Drunk on History   62

The Boy on the Couch   77

A Taste of Honey   92

The Wheat from the Tares   102

Planning the Perfect Evening   117

Lives of the Artists   126

Doo-wop   136

A Virtuous Woman   146

Ashes to Ashes   161

Grand Opening   172

Day Work   184

Burning Desires   194

Tahitian Treat   203

A Taste
of
Honey

I'd Rather Go Blind

$t$he summer of '67 was hot and foreboding. Folks in our neighborhood milled in the steamy streets, sweat-soaked and frowning. It was even hotter elsewhere: While other cities boiled over, Gateway mostly simmered. There was no question, though, that the temperature was steadily rising. Young men no longer hailed each other with an innocuous wave; instead they thrust black fists skyward. "Brothers and sisters are getting fed up," my brother Ed grew fond of saying. "Sooner or later some shit's gonna *explode.*" And it did.

Everybody had nicknames where we lived. People had two, three, sometimes four or five of them. If you didn't go to school or church with a kid, you could go your whole life without ever knowing what his real name was. A family on Greer Ave. had children known forever as Pumpkin, Pie, Buggy, and Cricket. Down the street from them was a kid called Boy, who was plenty nice as kids go. His real name was Dante, but not even his grandmother called him that. The kid on the corner of my block usually went by Man. Only occasionally was he called Roebuck Roundtree III. On the rest of our block we had two Peteys, a Tootie, a Decky, Big Wen and Big Hen, Throttles, and Choo-Choo. The tall, lean kid across the alley was named Lee but also answered to Bosco or Skillet.

The girls on our street had it just as bad. We had Twin, Boo,

Sissy, Yogi, Baa-Baa, and another Tootie, this one a big-legged girl from Clarksdale. Her real name was Parthinias.

Ed, seventeen and universally recognized as the Coolest Dude on Earth, was the sole exception to the multiple nickname game. The other kids simply called him Ed, each of them pronouncing his name with an audible note of awe, as if they were saying Supreme Commander or Your Royal Highness.

During the summer of '67, Ed was going through changes, my mother would say with a hint of impatience. He tended to mumble on the phone or talk in this deep grunt punctuated by the occasional "Right on" or mysterious reference to "the people." His friends joined him in an elaborate ritual of respect each time they saw each other, a semi-embrace full of handshakes, finger locks, and elbow bumps. Just as dramatically, these same old friends, known in the recent past by such affectionate names as Knucklehead and Punk Ass, became Brothers, as in

"If Brother Charles calls, tell him I'm on my way."

"If that's Brother Vaughn, tell him he knows where to find me."

My other brother, Schomburg, was twelve years old and impossible to live with. His nicknames were all flattering, owing to his easygoing grace and charming good looks—qualities that I couldn't bring myself to acknowledge, despite my best efforts. Girls called him Dimples. Boys called him Slick or Cool Breeze. Pop, who called me Hamburger, called him Superstar. Shom got that one from his coach and Little League teammates the night he hit three homers and gunned down the tying run at the plate from deep in right field. None of his admirers had any idea how obnoxious he could be in the privacy of his own room, which happened to be my room too.

There was no clearly marked border dividing our respective halves, but the contrast between the sides was so stark that a line may as well have been painted right down the middle. Shom liked to pretend that there was in fact a boundary, one made of dirt. There was no dust or debris on his side, little evidence that anyone even inhabited it. Everything reflected its owner's clearly neurotic obsession with neatness. All of his clothes were crisply folded and tucked tidily out of sight, save a red plaid robe hanging from a hook on the back of the door. Next to the door and leaning against the wall was a tall mirror, Shom's best friend.

He could stand in front of that thing for hours, it seemed to me. I suspected that he kept checking his reflection to reassure himself and smile away his worst fear: that his creamy brown complexion, dimples, and curls had just been part of a tantalizing dream. Like Ed, Shom was born handsome and appreciated the blessing. Still, he regarded the upkeep of his appearance as a sacred responsibility. Hence a good chunk of each day was spent maintaining his appearance, the better to solicit the compliments that he had come to expect as his birthright. He kept his comb and brush next to his bed, sometimes sleeping with them as if they were stuffed animals. I was never allowed to even handle his brush, and using it was out of the question. After all, science had yet to prove that nappy hair wasn't contagious.

I had no use for the mirror myself, certain that Shom's reflection would linger there to remind me tauntingly of all the things I lacked. I could let whole seasons go by without once glancing in that infernal glass.

It was my misfortune to be somewhat melanin-deprived just on the eve of the Black Is Beautiful revolution. I was yellow, beige on my best days, with orange lips that were big and swollen as Tweety Bird's beak. My hair was coppery with edges burned orange by the sun and locks coiled tight as bedsprings. My naps were stubborn yet soft as dust, although this latter quality didn't discourage the neighborhood kids from calling me Beanshots. No one really knew what beanshots were, but it was common playground parlance for extremely kinky hair. As a bonus, it was fun to pronounce and conveyed the unmistakable sting of insult.

My mother, Pristine, would never do such a dastardly thing as call me Beanshots, but she was clearly disappointed with my hair. She'd look at it with her lips pursed and her head turned slightly sideways, as if trying to figure out how things had gone wrong. My brother Ed had wavy hair that he cultivated by sleeping in a stocking cap and regularly applying generous doses of Murray's pomade. For all Shom's fussing with a comb and brush, all he really had to do was shake his head a little bit and every lock fell into place.

Mornings my mother met me with a sigh. She'd grip my chin firmly with one hand, then slap my face twice with the other to remind me to keep still. This was just before the hair-care market expanded to include Afro picks, and fine-tooth combs were absolute impossibilities, so she'd brush until her wrist got tired, then send me off to school. My scalp tingled and throbbed until lunchtime, when I would head home to eat and undergo the torture all over again. One of the reasons I liked summer so much was that Mom eased up on my hair, and the summer of '67 was no different. She'd let me go nappy for days at a time, and I'd be happy and headache-free.

Shom called me Beanshots only when other kids were around. In the privacy of our room, he preferred Pickle-Headed Pisspot (I tended to wet the bed) or his favorite, Big-headed Redheaded Monkey. He denies it now, says I'm prone to remembering things that never happened. I know what I heard, despite what he says. Some stuff just sticks with you.

Of all my nicknames, my favorite was Sir Crispus, a noble-sounding designation better suited to a valiant knight than to an ugly duckling. The only person who called me that was Curly, the short, scary-looking blind man who ran the candy store on Vandeventer, between the dry cleaners and the shoeshine parlor. I have no idea how he got his nickname, for his hair was anything but. In fact, his wild salt-and-pepper mane even gave me a run for my money—and he had a beard to match. He wore big, red-tinted sunglasses over eyes that I imagined were blank and wildly unfocused, rolling uncontrollably in their sockets. Rumor had it that Curly had traded his eyes to our neighborhood undertaker in exchange for the money to open his business.

He looked like he slept in his clothes and probably often did, on the cot in the little room behind the store that he called home. Sometimes we woke him when we ran to his store at lunchtime, eager to stuff ourselves with Lemonheads, Sugar Babies, Slo Pokes, and Chick-O-Sticks before the second bell. He'd rise, groaning and scratching yet moving effortlessly from the back room to the counter, where we clamored frantically for our daily dose of sugar. We wondered how his fingers knew just where to find the brand of candy we demanded, how he made correct change without hesitation. More than a few kids agreed with Bumpy Decatur when he insisted that Curly wasn't blind at all but merely engaged in some complicated scam. Curly dubbed me Sir Crispus the Pure-Hearted when, against the advice of the two Peteys and Choo-Choo, I'd returned the extra Now and Laters he'd accidentally placed in my bag.

I saw more of Curly on days when I hung out with Father Time, whose grandparents ran the cleaners next door to the candy shop. Father Time, christened Brian by his unwitting parents, was so nicknamed because of the slow way he walked and talked. We'd take turns tossing a rubber ball against the wall of the cleaners while his grandfather Mr. Kirkwood kept an eye on us. I loved to watch the old man operate his big steam press, the way he ignored the massive cloud of mist that seemed to always encircle his head. When business was lagging Curly would sit on the stoop behind his store and listen to records. Usually it was the same one: "I'd Rather Go Blind." He'd nod his head behind his red shades, a cigarette turning to ash between his bony fingers. "Etta James," he'd say. "She ain't got no idea."

There was a calendar on Curly's wall with a naked woman on it. Father Time and I had made it our mission to tiptoe past the nodding Curly and make out her mysterious curves in the dim recesses of his room. But every time we tried, we would hear, "Shame on you, Sir Crispus," as if he was reading my mind. "Sneaking a peek at another man's woman."

"Sorry," I'd apologize. "You mean she's—?"

"That's right. Miss June. Used to be mine, for sure. And once you been Curly's, you cain't be nobody else's. Sir Crispus, you too young to even know what I'm talking about."

For a long time we kids used to wonder where Curly hid his dog during the day. Father Time and I never saw any evidence of the huge beast that we knew lurked somewhere in Curly's tiny lair, along with his cot, his calendar, and his record player. At night, however, the dog's loud, piercing wails could be heard as far away as Natural Bridge Boulevard, four blocks distant.

One night I asked my dad if he'd ever seen Curly's dog.

"What dog?"

"The one that's howling right now. Don't you hear it?"

My mom's mom, who preferred to be called Big Mama but whom I secretly nicknamed the Grandmother, was visiting from her home down the block. She snorted.

"That's an animal all right," she said, "but it's not a dog."

"Be nice, Big Mama," Mom cautioned.

The Grandmother waved her hand. "Just telling it like it is."

"That's Curly you hear," Dad explained. "Sometimes he drinks too much rotgut and it forces all his anger out."

"His gut isn't the only thing that's rotting," the Grandmother said. "His soul can't be far behind."

I had no worries about Curly's soul. Only a good man could have the uncanny ability to emerge from his storefront just when Bumpy Decatur and his brothers were about to shake us down for our candy money. Only a good man would forbid the other kids to call me Beanshots in his presence. "That's Sir Crispus," he'd declare. "He's got history in his name. You little whippersnappers need to get some respect."

I sensed instinctively that he was not a corrupt man, merely a sad one. His tale, which Father Time and I caught in whiskey-soaked fragments muttered between verses of Etta James, was too involved for a boy of nine to get his imagination around. Even so, I knew it involved missed opportunities, a beautiful woman, and a broken heart. What more was there to know?

One night in early June, Curly's mysterious past was consigned to smoke and ashes forever.

Shom and I were already bathed and in our pajamas, watching *Mr. Terrific*, when the quiet of evening gave way to the sound of shattering glass. Shouts, curses, and sirens followed. My father leaned out of my parents' bedroom window on the second floor. "Someone's down," my father said. "A lot of people are gathering on the corner. Maybe I—"

"Maybe you should shut that window and sit down," my mother said. "Nothing but trouble out there."

There was a knock at the door. My father went down to answer it, my mother close at his heels. Shom and I peeked through the upstairs banister. "It's Collins," Pop said. He opened the door.

Mr. Collins, our next-door neighbor, skipped his usual greetings.

"Reuben, let's go down to the corner," he said.

"Why's that?"

Mr. Collins hesitated, then shot a quick glance at my mother before returning his gaze to Pop. "Is Ed here?"

Pristine gasped. My father looked at her, and then rushed past Mr. Collins. Our neighbor looked apologetically at my mom. "Don't worry," he said. He left and shut the door.

"Lord have mercy," my mother whispered. She called Shom and me and gathered us in her arms.

We huddled in silence while confusion swirled loudly outside. *Mr. Terrific* went off. I wanted to get up and change the channel to NBC because it was time for my favorite show, *Captain Nice*. I could almost hear its opening theme: "That's no ordinary nut, boy, that's Captain Nice!"

The door swung open. Ed stepped in, followed by my dad. Ed had a small cut on his forehead. My mother ran to him, her arms spread wide.

"Baby," she said.

Ed held her. "I'm fine, Mom. I'm fine."

She stared at his wound. "Did the police do that?"

"No, Mom. The people were throwing all kinds of stuff out there. I think some glass caught me." To my eyes Ed looked changed, battle-scarred somehow. I wondered if a piece of glass could make so much difference.

"It was just a handful of folks making a whole lotta fuss," my dad said. "It's over, at least for now. The police are gone. They've done enough damage tonight."

"Jesus, Ed," Mom said. "Mr. Collins came by and told us you were out there. I was so afraid."

Dad put his hand on Ed's shoulder. "Tell your mom what happened."

My father slid the piano bench over so that Ed could sit down, but Ed seemed not to notice. "It was the three of us," he began.

"Brother Vaughn, Brother Charles, and me. Walking down Vandeventer and not bothering anybody. Out of nowhere, these cops come up and start giving us a hard time. Right there at the corner. If I had wanted to, I could have seen the TV light blinking in y'all's window. But I kept my eyes on these two cops. One of them was Ray Mortimer."

Mom gasped at the name, because everyone knew that Mortimer was just plain bad news.

"I didn't say anything," Ed continued, "but Vaughn, well, he and Mortimer got into some words. He pushed Vaughn and moved his hand toward his gun. Then Curly comes out of his store, shouting something at them. The cops turned toward him and we ran. We leaped over the shrubs on the corner and ran down the gangway. We thought the cops might follow us, but Curly kept hollering, like he was trying to distract them. We came around the other side of the shoeshine parlor and peeked from behind the wall. Mortimer came toward Curly flipping his nightstick. We heard him tell Curly, 'Mind your business, you blind fool.'

"Curly grinned and said, 'I may be blind but I have seen the light. Have you?'

"The cop slapped the nightstick into the palm of his hand. 'You looking for trouble, wino?'

" 'No sir,' Curly said. 'I'm looking for an honest man.'

"Mortimer shoved Curly in the chest. 'Keep walking, old coon,' he said."

Policemen had a nickname too, just like the rest of us. Theirs is seldom heard these days, but it was just becoming popular back then. It made some cops mad to hear it; it made others crazy. Curly must have known he was taking a chance.

" 'Of course,' Curly said, 'I guess an honest *pig* is even harder to find.' "

Ed went to the window next to the piano and stared outside. He took a deep breath. "Mortimer let loose with his nightstick. Curly seemed to smile, like he knew it was coming and was getting ready to duck. I hoped for a miracle, that Curly would suddenly have sight. But he stayed blind and he almost walked right into it. It was just a glancing blow, but hard enough to topple him. Curly fell and hit the back of his head on the curb. 'That you, Miss June?' he said. 'Well, it's about time.' "

Ed turned to my mother. "What do you think he meant?"

Mom wiped her eyes. "It doesn't matter," she said. "He's at peace now. His soul's at rest."

I knew what Curly meant, although I didn't let on. And I knew what I had to do.

Since Curly had no family, our neighborhood took up a collection to give him a proper going away. The funeral was for grown folks. While they all sang and mourned in Good Samaritan Methodist Church, I talked Father Time into borrowing the key that Curly had given his grandparents for safekeeping. Father Time stood guard while I let myself in. I climbed onto Curly's shaky cot and pulled Miss June from the wall. I respectfully looked away while placing her in a bag.

"Hold on, Crisp," Father Time said. "Shouldn't we at least look at those titties?"

"Shame on you," I said. "Sneaking a peek at another man's woman. It ain't right."

I took the Etta James record for myself. Curly had once told me that I was sure to get my heart broken someday. When that time came, he said, it was best to have some Etta on hand to ease my pain.

Father Time accompanied me to Fairgrounds Park. He watched while I put a stone in the bag with the calendar, sealed it with a rubber band, and tossed it into the lake. "Damn, Beanshots," he said. "This is crazy."

I smiled as the bag disappeared into the lake's muddy depths.

"You ain't got no idea," I said.

Something Like God

*O*utside Curly's funeral at Good Samaritan Methodist Church, men of purpose gathered. Dark glasses hid their eyes. Their unsmiling mouths were firmly set except when words like *brutality* and *revolution* fell from their lips. "Off the pigs" was their heartfelt refrain. Ten men strong, they paraded beneath the watchful gaze of their leader, Gabriel "the Liberator" Patterson.

Inside Good Samaritan, something wondrous was going on. What had been a home-going for a blind man became another thing entirely, floating on waves of unearthly sound. Pristine Jones rocked in her seat and smiled. She was rocking, yes, but she rocked all the time, didn't she? If anyone knew how to praise the Lord, it was Pristine. She sneaked a glance at her husband. Even Reuben was tapping his toes in spite of himself. His buddies from Black Swan Sign Shop—Bob Cobb, George West, Lucius Monday, even Talk Much—the bittersweet rhythm shook them all.

Rev. Miles Washington, hardly a young man, hadn't aged for years. He was black and burnished. A scar running down the side of his neck and into his collar hurt his beauty not in the least. He was sending Rex Canada home.

Curly hadn't answered to Rex since he was knee-high to a grasshopper. He came to town as Curly, simply Curly. Like many black men of his generation, he'd come north hungry and hurried, tight-lipped and lean. Little in his pockets and even less to say about where he had been and what sent him. The Kirkwoods, owners of the dry cleaners and the little hole in the wall where Curly lived and worked, had been the only folks who knew his real name. And they didn't know much beyond that.

No matter, for Curly was beyond hearing. His sightless eyes were closed, his shades tucked into his breast pocket. With beard trimmed and wild mane tamed, he was threatening handsome. People who had passed him on the street for decades wouldn't have recognized him.

Rev. Washington was going on like he liked to do, and Pristine loved him for it. He revealed the wisdom of the word, with Rose Whittier humming underneath it all. As the reverend's voice rode on Rose's hypnotic melisma, Pristine realized what folks meant when they said "on the wings of song." She looked around and saw many strangers, folks who'd come to witness for themselves the latest poor soul sent to glory by Gateway City police. "He might as well have stayed in Mississippi," Reuben had said that morning. But who knew where Curly was from?

All that mattered to Rev. Washington was where he was going.

"Anybody can get there," he was saying. "You just have to ask and the gates of Zion will be thrown open to you. Are we not all sinners? Yes, we are. My Lord, we have all sinned against thee. But we believe—we know—we can all be saved by your grace."

Rose stood in front of the mourners, eyes closed. Her humming rose and fell.

"Hear me, church? I don't think you do. Brother Canada had the courage to confront corruption. Brother Canada wasn't a rich man. He wasn't particularly large. And yet he stood in the face of wrong and spoke out against it. He paid with his body, but his soul is intact, brothers and sisters. He was faithful that, in the end, justice would roll down like a mighty stream. Let us honor Brother Canada by demonstrating our own faith. It takes courage to have faith. Let us likewise be brave, church. Be brave and believe. Dear Lord, we thank you for your bountiful love and ask safe passage for Brother Rex Canada as he heads to glory, over on that other shore."

Rose Whittier threw back her head. The sound seemed to come from everywhere at once. A miracle lived in her mouth.

I'm just a poor wayfaring stranger

"Amen," said Rev. Washington.

I'm traveling through this world of woe

"Amen, amen."

*O*utside Good Samaritan, Gabriel listened to one of his men go on and on, spitting mumbo jumbo—power, people, pigs, something. Gabriel silenced him with a wave of the hand.

"Listen," Gabriel said. It was not a suggestion.

But there's no sickness, toil or danger
In that bright land to which I go

The Warriors of Freedom stared at their leader. He paid them no mind.

I'm going there to see my father
I'm going there no more to roam
I'm just a-going over Jordan
I'm just a-going over home

Through the walls and windows of the church came a voice so lovely and pure it almost hurt to hear it. If the Liberator had not been careful, his soldiers might have seen him weep.

He took two steps toward the sound, stopped. He willed himself still. Gabriel made himself content to listen from where he was.

He had been busy throughout the region, organizing, strategizing, avoiding the eager gaze of the law. Love was not high on his list of priorities. Plenty of women had warmed his bed, but love? Gabriel was willing to die for freedom. To love, however, was to risk a different kind of hurt. It was foolish, almost as foolish as falling in love with just a voice. Get hold of yourself, he told himself. You haven't even seen her face.

Inside the church, Rose radiated joy. A slight sheen coated her plump, dimpled cheeks. Her head was still back, her arms open wide. Swaying slowly, she seemed unaware of the mourners, many of whom had never heard her before. Some were crying. A few began to dance in place. Others rose and swayed with her, clutching themselves tightly. Pristine was among the standing, waving a handkerchief above her head. Rose kept her eyes closed, as if opening them would break the spell.

Half a mile from Good Samaritan, Rose's husband, Paul Whittier, headed to Curly's funeral. Running late from running around, he really wanted to run away, but where would he go?

His mouth was dry and his pockets were empty. Every fat man he saw was looking like Guts Tolliver when an unmarked police car swelled into view and hovered in his rearview mirror. Paul pulled his prized baby blue Electra 225 to the curb. "I'll be goddamned," he said.

> *I'm going there to see my mother*
> *I'm going there no more to roam*

Tears filled Pristine's eyes as she listened. She recalled Ed telling the story of Curly's dying, his strange smile when he seemed to walk right into the blow. What were those broken eyes seeing just then? Pristine wondered. Ed had said something about a woman named June. Curly's mother, maybe. She looked at Rose, whose eyes were closed tight. We should hear her in church more often, Pristine decided. Too bad Paul was so jealous of her gifts, she thought. I wonder what Rose sees right now.

"You want to come on out of the car, son?"

Paul unwound all of his six feet, one inch from behind the wheel, slowly got out, and stood at the mercy of Detective Ray Mortimer.

"That's quite a vehicle you got here, Paul Whittier."

Paul said nothing, squinted into the sun. He was beginning to think he might miss Rose singing. Maybe it was for the best.

"Where I'm from that's called a compliment."

Paul stared in the direction of the church. "Where I'm from," he said, "it's called a deuce and a quarter."

It was Detective Mortimer's turn to squint. Every day he seemed to run into a different kind of Negro. What kind was this?

"You mocking me, son?"

"No, sir, not at all." Paul struggled to contain his disgust.

"What do you do, Paul Whittier?" Each time he read Paul's name from his driver's license, as if he couldn't say it without the help the letters provided.

"Officer, I don't mean any disrespect, but I'm expected at church—"

Church, Mortimer thought. Figures. Now every Tom, Dick, and Leroy thinks he's Martin Luther King. "You a preacher or something?"

"No, sir. I'm a singer."

"No shit? Me too. I'm a regular Pat Boone. What's the name of your group?"

"The Whittier Brothers Quartet."

"Doo-wop, I bet. I love that stuff. The Ink Spots, the Four Tops. Crazy about it, if you can imagine."

"I sing gospel," Paul said.

"Oh," said Mortimer, taking another admiring look at Paul's Buick. "Too bad. You make a living doing that?"

"I work at the Chevy plant too."

"No shit? Hey, the old cruiser's been acting strange all day. Mind takin' a look?"

Paul shook his head. "Like I said, I got someplace to be."

Mortimer stared a long minute at Paul. Then he cackled, loud and shrill. Paul trembled in spite of himself.

*G*ood Samaritan wanted to be known as a helping hands church. Its reputation in this regard was capably enhanced by the steadfast humanitarian efforts of members like Pristine, who were constantly involved in various relief and charity campaigns. Still, despite its annual Christmas gala for Annie

Malone's Children's Home, regular contributions to the Southern Christian Leadership Conference, and its pastor serving as a volunteer chaplain at the North Side's only public hospital, it was still referred to by many as "the gangster's church."

Reuben Jones often called it that, but he always made sure that Pristine was far away when he did. His colleagues from Black Swan Sign Shop also called it the gangster's church, although they, like Reuben, knew that the gangster's name—Ananias Goode—appeared nowhere on Good Samaritan's papers. At the same time, they knew better than others that his handiwork was everywhere, in the light-filled reception hall, the mammoth pipe organ, just about any place an eagle-eyed believer turned.

"The gangster" was one of the North Side's best-known and most colorful figures and, as might be expected, no stranger to controversy. Although heartily feared and despised by much of Gateway's colored aristocracy, Goode was admired by many of his less fortunate brethren, as much for his bodacious style as for his obvious sense of comfort. He didn't behave as if he belonged in the world; he conducted himself as if the world belonged to him. Lately he had wrapped himself even more deeply in the good graces of the poor by way of several timely and enthusiastically publicized acts of generosity. He cut an impressive figure, for instance, in that week's *Gateway Citizen*, standing next to the alderman from the fifth ward at the groundbreaking for the new Harry Truman Boys' Club.

Jowly and chocolate-skinned, Goode was a loan shark and self-described small business owner, but nothing about him appeared to be undersize. His face was big in an impressive way: a pair of bristly brows sprouting wildly above expansive eyes that seemed to miss nothing; broad African nostrils; thick, proud lips; strong teeth usually holding an expensive-looking cigar in a death clench. The head sat atop an equally stout body, which he kept clad in banker's pinstripes and custom-made shoes. He'd never set foot in Good Samaritan, but his New Yorker was often seen idling at the curb during the last days of construction. He'd sit in the backseat thumbing the *Wall Street Journal* or the *Racing Form* while his chief leg-breaker, Guts Tolliver, sat behind the miniature steering wheel, special-ordered to accommodate his capacious girth.

Reuben was not a habitual churchgoer, but he knew Good Samaritan almost as well as Pristine did. He and the men of the Black Swan had done all the interior and exterior painting. In addition, Reuben had carved the altarpiece and the bas-relief biblical scenes adorning the chapel doors. The stained-glass portrait of black Jesus behind the pulpit was based on a design by Lucius Monday. (The pastor's sole decorating contribution was his strange insistence that an arrow, mounted on a plaque like a hunting trophy, be positioned in the central place of honor on the wall behind his desk.) Rev. Washington neither blinked nor faltered when Reuben outlined his plans to him, not even when Reuben told him about the gold leaf needed for the altarpiece. He sent the men of the Black Swan to see Ana-nias Goode, who in turn quadrupled Reuben's account at Brod-Dugan Paints and Supplies.

Reuben's men were briefly flush, a development that led to a new baby for George West and enabled Lucius to move out of Reuben's garage and into a room at Mrs. Williams's boarding-house.

Goode struck Reuben as the kind of man who could see at least a couple days into the future if not more, who would know the punch line before you began the joke. Occasionally, Reuben was summoned to the big man's car to provide an update on his crew's work. Reuben eventually grew comfortable (or at least considerably less apprehensive) during these interviews, typically conducted through Goode's half-opened window, from which exuded a blend of cigar smoke, horehound drops, and Old Spice.

A favorite game among North Siders, one not limited to notorious gossips such as Pristine's mother, involved speculation regarding the connection between Rev. Washington and Ananias Goode. (The guessing game was stimulated by a reliable source's solemn assertion that an arrow, the very twin of the reverend's peculiar trophy, was similarly displayed in Goode's lair.) Most of the talk suggested that Goode owed Washington a debt that could never be paid in full, but neither man divulged a thing. The pastor never hid his fondness for Goode, nor did he refrain from condemning his misdeeds. The chief and most durable rumor was a shadowy tale of death defiance down South, when the two men were just youngsters. Ananias Goode escaped with his life, the story went, and Rev. Washington came away with a scar.

To Reuben the scar appeared to pulsate as Rev. Washington reacted to Rose's heavenly voice. The men of the Black Swan were as vulnerable to idle talk as anyone else, and some nights after a case of Stag had been consumed (by all but Lucius, who instead inhaled several cups of White Castle coffee sweetened with cheap Rosie O'Grady wine), one painter or another ventured the opinion that the devout Rev. Washington had once been a gangster too, and might even still be one.

Reuben cast such thoughts aside as he glanced at his wife standing and swaying next to him. Rose was winding down, and her voice would soon give way in Pristine's consciousness to her three boys. Reuben knew Pristine would start to worry about them, despite his earlier reassurances. Ed was working a double shift at SuperMart, stocking groceries and stuffing bags.

Shom, in the temporary and admiring custody of Coach Alphin, was at Sherman Park holding down right field for the undefeated Roadrunners. Crisp was at the Kirkwoods' (who didn't do funerals), playing with their grandson Brian and—God willing, as Pristine often said—staying out of trouble.

*R*ose responded politely to all the well-wishers who praised her after Curly's funeral. She even squeezed a hand or two and accepted—briefly—some pecks on the cheek, all the while moving toward the exit with deliberate speed. "I appreciate that, but I really have to go," she said. "I'm looking for my— Oh, thank you, kindly. Have you seen my— Yes, yes, God bless you too." At last she reached the doorway. Where was Paul?

Gabriel, as it turned out, was also thinking about a Paul. As Rose stepped onto the porch of the church, dimpled and demure in her modest dress and summer hat, Gabriel felt a sudden and unexpected sympathy for the man who fell off his ass on the way to Damascus. Like that legendary apostle, Gabriel had been slapped silly by a vision.

He noted a change in his perception, the world whirling differently against his senses. The small talk and hubbub faded to white noise, a dull hissing. Grass, sky, buildings, and people all fell away into empty space and silence, leaving only *her,* the woman with the voice. Somehow he knew: she was the one.

"Have mercy," he said softly.

He saw *inside* Rose, past fabric and flesh to the warmth within. There he saw time turning upon time, mysteries and constellations giving shape to children, beautiful children—*his* children, growing and sprouting in there. Something was bothering him, buzzing at his ears. A mosquito? A bee? He batted at it, never taking his eyes off Rose as she slowly descended the stairs, looking left and right. But it didn't go away. A wasp? A fly? PeeWee Jefferson, one of his Warriors. With a stack of leaflets in his hand.

"Commander, shouldn't we be giving these out?"

"Right. Hand 'em out. Right on."

Gabriel's men fanned out and began to distribute the leaflets as they had been trained.

"Good day, brother. Good day, sister," they began in velvet tones. "We are the Warriors of Freedom and we would like to invite you to a rally . . ."

The leaflets they dispensed asked the questions whispered in barbershops and shoeshine parlors and beauty salons all over the North Side. They were printed in bold black ink, surrounding the crosshaired image of a pig wearing a policeman's hat: "How many good brothers must die before this bloody trend is reversed? Isn't it time we offed the pigs?"

Meanwhile, where to begin? Come live with me and be my love? Hell, no. Can I walk you home? Negro, please. After testing and discarding an overture or two, the Liberator made his move.

"Sister, may I have a minute of your time? We could sure use a voice like yours."

Rose looked up to see a thin, brown-skinned man in army fatigues. His lips were full and sensitive; a wispy goatee coated his chin. She couldn't see the eyes hidden behind his dark glasses, but he seemed handsome in a starving-poet kind of way. His back was strong and straight, and his hands looked quite capable. But his belt, wrapped nearly two times around his waist, was barely holding his pants up.

"I only sing for the Lord, sir." Rose thought she should keep moving. Where was Paul?

"The Lord's got plenty of angels he can count on, sister.

The Warriors, on the other hand, we need all the help we can get. You oughta sing for us, sister. I'm sorry, I didn't catch your name."

"It's Rose. Rose Whittier."

"Sister Rose. Like the rose of Sharon."

Rose cupped her hand above her brow to shield her eyes from the sun, but it was an affectation. Her hat was doing that job. She stole a glance at the man. He looked hungry. "You know the Word," she said.

"O my dove," said Gabriel, "that art in the clefts of the rock, in the secret places of the stairs, let me see thy countenance, let me hear thy voice; for sweet is thy voice, and thy countenance is comely."

Rose smiled. "You really know the Word."

"Why wouldn't I?"

"You didn't strike me as a man of faith."

Gabriel chuckled. "Judge not, my sister. I'm sure you know Luke."

"I apologize. I—"

"No need, no need. I'm the one who should be sorry, sorry for not meeting you years ago." He removed his glasses and extended his hand. His eyes looked surprisingly hopeful to Rose, sort of hazel, with flakes of gold. "Patterson, Gabriel. Also known as the Liberator."

Rose left him hanging. "Should I call you Mr. Patterson or Mr. Liberator?"

"How about Gabriel?"

"I don't think so. I'm a married woman, Mr. Patterson."

"Of course you are." He frowned, regained his composure, lost it again.

Rose watched, embarrassed, as the Liberator appeared to argue with himself. "Stupid," he muttered. "Shoulda checked for a ring. See what you get for thinking maybe this happened for a reason. Something like fate. Something like God. You silly, silly fool."

He snapped out of it. "Forgive me," he said, replacing his glasses with a snap. "If I could just impose upon you with a leaflet, then. We rally weekends at Franklin and Jefferson. Please join us when you can." Their hands touched briefly when Rose reached for the leaflet. She felt heat rise in her cheeks.

In time she tired of waiting. She rode home with the Joneses, climbed the stairs to her lonely flat. The leaflet, meant to be disposed of hours before, sat on the table next to the phone. As the day gave way to dusk, Rose played some Aretha and put Paul's dinner in the oven to keep it warm.

The leaflet would catch Paul's eye later that night as he stomped through the narrow hallway, his chronic anger coming on. Glaring through his half-drunken haze at the swollen hog in a policeman's hat, Paul would remember the humiliation he'd suffered earlier that day at the hands of Detective Mortimer. He would recall the way that disgusting pig had made him shuffle and sweat like he had all the time in the world. How the cop had made him stand lookout while he pissed all over Paul's just-polished chrome. Seeing the leaflet would bring it all back: While he was kissing a cracker's ass, Rose was shaking hers in front of the folks at that blind fool's funeral. Paul would then remind her, as he often did, to keep her ass to herself.

Sweet Rose would pay for Mortimer's arrogance. She would pay for her beauty and the voice that matched it. She would pay for Paul's career struggles and his trifling brothers, who seldom got to rehearsal on time or sober. She would pay for imagined flirtations. She would pay like her Lord paid, with welts and thorns and bruises and the taste of blood in her mouth.

It would end as it always ended, with Paul crying and Rose whimpering quietly. He would yank her from the floor, where she had curled into a ball, her head and shoulders crammed under the bed or the bureau. He would force her to her knees and make her pray beside him.

"I don't want to," she would say, quietly. "Please. Please don't make me."

"It's not for me," he would say through his tears. "It's for Jesus. He wants you to know I'm sorry. He wants you to forgive me."

But that was hours away yet. Right then a warm breeze was tickling Rose's face and a handsome stranger had just made her blush. The sun danced through the leaves and dappled the afternoon with bright flakes of gold, outside Good Samaritan.

Zombies

*S*oon after my mom finally agreed to let me cross the street by myself, I forgot to look both ways while returning home and was nearly blindsided by a fast-moving Ford Fairlane. I escaped harm, though, until I reached our front porch. That's when Pristine pulled me inside and commenced to clobbering me with the closest thing handy—a flip-flop that seconds before had been dangling from her foot. For a brief, merciful moment I was able to break free. I wrenched open the screen door and lunged for the porch, but Mom caught me by the ankles. Across the street, Petey and Choo-Choo bore astonished witness to the strange sight of me disappearing backward through the front door, an invisible force sucking me in like I was one of those anonymous doomed crewmen in a *Star Trek* episode. They got a final glimpse of my tear-streaked, horrified face frozen in midyell before it vanished behind the screen door.

Afterward, Petey told me that all he could make out through the mesh was the dim outline of my mother and "that flip-flop going up and down, up and down."

Buttwhippings were a common sight back then. Dal Frederick used to get thrashed from one end of our long block to the other about once a week. Lucky Simpson's mom used to come looking for him with an ironing cord draped around her shoulders like a mink stole. Even so, when a buttwhipping goes public, it takes a while for the whippee to live it down. Folks called me Flip-Flop for weeks.

Mom banned me from leaving the front lawn unaccompanied. The upside: my brother Schomburg had to escort me everywhere, including to and from school when it resumed that fall. The downside: I had to follow wherever he led, and his curious path to school always wound past Burk's Funeral Home—just about the last place on earth that I wanted to be near. Shom knew this, and resenting my unavoidable presence at his side, he determined to punish me each morning. He took the long way, turning the corner at Vandeventer, sauntering past Teenie's Lounge, and pausing to look for discarded bottle tops outside Hudson's Package Liquor before crossing Ashland Ave. to walk by Burk's.

The place didn't bother me until I came to realize there were *dead bodies* inside. Shom never failed to remind me of this grisly fact on our way to Farragut Elementary. Sometimes he made spooky, baying sounds as we passed its darkened windows, *woo-woo*s teasing the back of my neck. Other times he'd laugh like Dracula and swear that the unfortunate folks who lived on Ashland had to put up with the sounds of corpses stirring about at night, banging on windows and scratching at doors. Once in a while Shom would stop and say, "Shhh. Did you hear that?"

"H-hear what?"

He'd put his hand to his ear. "Sounded like scratching."

My bladder always swelled when I got scared. Or maybe it shrank.

"Don't tell me you don't hear that, Crisp."

Then Shom would look over my shoulder in mock horror. "Oh my God," he'd gasp. "Run!"

It got me every time. He'd take off flying with me running behind him crying and stumbling, dropping my Captain Nice lunch box and refusing to go back and get it. Shom would put on the brakes near the end of the block, his All Stars skidding on the bumpy sidewalk. After laughing and catching his breath, he'd suddenly get serious and become disgusted with me. He knew that no amount of argument would persuade me to go get that lunch box, so he'd stomp back and retrieve it. We'd proceed in sullen silence, Shom keeping the lunch box until we reached the entrance to the school playground.

Shom would go through the gates and sit my lunch box on a hopscotch grid.

"You're a punk, you know that?"

"Am not."

" 'Am not.' Listen to you. Remember, you don't know me."

He'd spin on his heels and strut over to the seventh-grade portables, where he was a line monitor and a big shot.

That was on school days. When summer vacation came in '67, I was able to go weeks without having to think of Burk's, much less go near it. One July day, I finagled an invite to Shom's baseball practice. I had talked my mom nearly under the table, irritating her so much that she bribed Shom to take me along. On the way back from the park we stopped at Chink's with Flukey Williams, the team's fast-talking shortstop. He was so cool that he took infield grounders wearing Hush Puppies and a Big Apple cap.

Chink's was the confectionery on Lexington, across the alley from Burk's. Flukey bought a bag of barbecued Fiesta corn chips and a sixteen-ounce bottle of Vess Orange Whistle. It was the most popular soda in those days, although I preferred Tahitian Treat myself. Shom got ten oatmeal cookies for himself and a sour apple Bub's Daddy for me. In exchange I agreed not to talk for a whole block.

The deal seemed easy enough. As we strolled along I imagined myself in my room, reclining in front of the fan smacking away at my gum, green-tongued and lazily adrift on a daydream. Until a voice startled me.

"Afternoon, boys."

It was Mr. Burk. He was fond of sitting outside on hot days, waving at passersby and catching catnaps in his wide porch chair. His building had no porch to speak of, just a stoop. He sat yards in front of that, near the edge of the sidewalk. The front door of Burk's faced the street on a diagonal, and there was no parking lot at all. An alley ramp led to double doors in the back, through which the bodies were brought in. Mr. Burk shared an apartment above the parlor with his creepy son, Austin, whom I felt a little sorry for. I couldn't begin to imagine actually having to go to sleep above a bunch of dead people, especially dead people who liked to get up and go places at night. Mr. Burk was a round man, from the top of his bald brown dome, past the crest of his bulbous belly, down to his shoes, which had round knob toes. None of that made him bad-looking or even scary, however. His voice was kindly enough, and he even reminded me of pictures I'd seen of the man who used to sing with Count Basie's band, the man my father fondly called Mr. Five by Five. It was Mr. Burk's eyes that gave most of us trouble.

We kids were used to unusual eyes and as a matter of course bestowed suitable nicknames upon folks who had them. Shade Eye had a muscle problem that made one lid droop. Beer Eyes had peepers that were unnaturally yellow. There was even a pair of light-skinned twins who lived near the Catholic school and were known as Green Eyes and Brown Eyes. Mr. Burk's eyeballs were a cloudy gray and strangely glassy, so we called him Zombie Eyes. Behind his back, of course.

"Hi, Mr. Burk," Shom said.

"Hey, Mr. Burk," said Flukey.

I nodded, remembering my bargain with Shom. Mr. Burk leaned forward and looked at me. With his face so close to mine, it was hard to avoid his eyes. They were cloudy as always and looked hard as glass. I didn't wonder how they ended up like that. I already knew how, and I also knew that they were fake. They were fake and yet he could still see.

I don't know exactly who started the rumor, but it was confirmed by the fifteen Finger kids, who lived two doors west of Burk's. One day at recess, they told us it was true that the fat funeral director dealt in the underground eye market.

"Haven't you noticed how little white folks' eyes are?" Eric Finger asked.

"Yeah," Big Hen said. "They do have some little bitty eyes."

A bunch of boys were sitting on the rail surrounding the swings on the playground. Being a little kid, I hung around in back, but close enough to hear everything. The white person I was most familiar with was Ed Sullivan, and I had to agree: he had tiny eyes.

"Well," Eric said. "They like to buy black folks' eyes because ours are so much bigger and better-looking. You know how rich white folks are. When black folks die they pay for their eyes. Mr. Burk's been dealing for a long time. He takes the eyes out the bodies and keeps 'em in a cooler in the back. Late at night a white dude comes by and takes 'em out in a metal box."

Big Hen shook his head. "That's messed up, man. People's gettin' buried without they eyes."

"Yeah," Eric said. "He puts marbles in and nobody notices because the eyelids are sewed shut."

"Wait a minute," Big Hen said. "What about Miss Gordon? She don't have little eyes."

Miss Gordon was the only white teacher at our school. Eric must have heard this question before.

"She used to when she first came here. Then when she came back from summer vacation, she had new eyes. I bet she bought 'em from old man Burk."

After absorbing Eric's wisdom, I brought my new knowledge to my oldest brother, Ed. He knew all about Burk.

"That's no secret," he said. "But it sounds like that Finger kid told you only half the story. The worst part was when Burk took this one dude's eyes out and put in marbles in their place. Turns out the dude was a zombie and he was really pissed when he woke up and found out what Burk had done. The old man had been sleeping when he heard a noise in the middle of the night. He opened his eyes and found the zombie standing right over him. They got to fighting, knocking over furniture and stuff. The two of them made so much noise that somebody ran across Vandeventer and pulled the firebox. It might have been Austin, because he took off butt naked, hotfooting it all the way to Fairgrounds Park."

I knew I would have trouble getting to sleep, but I had to hear it all. "Then what happened?"

"Nobody knows for sure. The firemen came with a lot of loud sirens and stuff, but it took them a while to get in the door. The zombie must have taken Burk's eyes and stuck the marbles in their place. The firemen found the old man on the floor blinking them strange gray eyes. The zombie was gone. They didn't find Austin until the next morning. He was way up a telephone pole, still naked and foaming at the mouth. They had to get him down with a cherry picker, and he stayed in the hospital for six weeks. He won't talk about that night."

"But how can Mr. Burk see with those marbles?"

Ed smiled. I appreciated how patient he was with me. He

was the only member of the family who never told me that I talked too much, and I loved him for that. "The zombie had the power to come back from the dead, right? That means he also had the power to make dead things live. When he touched the marbles, he gave them energy, and that energy is what makes Mr. Burk able to see."

$\mathcal{I}$t felt like Mr. Burk could see right through me when he leaned close. I wondered why he found me so interesting when Flukey was standing next to me in that cool Big Apple cap. "How about you, young man? Cat got your tongue?"

I shrugged helplessly and looked at Shom. "It's all right, Crispus," he said. "You can talk."

I didn't want to be rude, but I wanted no part of those eyes. So I concentrated on Mr. Burk's forehead. "I'm fine," I whispered.

He reached out and rubbed my head. The round man had square fingers and nails, like the characters in those Jack Kirby comic books that Ed used to love so much. His hand smelled strange, vaguely unnatural. He leaned back and addressed all of us.

"You kids want to see something interesting?"

"Like what?" Flukey asked.

"Like a dead body," Mr. Burk replied.

Flukey and Shom exchanged excited glances. "You got one in there right now?" Shom asked.

Mr. Burk nodded. "Cooling on the slab."

"Well, maybe just a little look," Shom said breathlessly.

The chair squeaked and groaned as Mr. Burk adjusted his bulk. Slowly he rose and gestured toward the door behind him. "After you," he said.

Flukey and Shom stepped toward the door. I remained where I was. Shom turned to me. "What?" I said.

"You coming?"

"Nope. I'm waiting right here." I folded my arms.

Shom turned and faced me so that Mr. Burk couldn't see his expression. "You're a punk," he hissed. "You know that, right?"

"Aw, leave him alone. Just wait right there, Crisp. We'll be right back."

I always liked Flukey. I hoped that I would get to see him again as I watched the three of them vanish into the darkness of the funeral parlor. I waited for what seemed like forever, shifting from one foot to the other and trying not to think about restless corpses or the fact that Flukey and Shom had such young, healthy-looking eyes. I pictured a man in a dusky parking lot, standing next to a car with an open trunk. The trunk contained a small metal box. A long line of rich white people were queuing up next to the car. A snotty-looking woman in fancy clothes was asking the man if he had anything in brown.

Flukey and Shom came out the door with a swagger.

"Nothing to it," Flukey said. He tugged his cap over his brow, grabbed his crotch, and spat a neat stream through the gap in his teeth. Cool.

Shom shaded his eyes with his hand, which disturbed me. I wanted to get a good look at them, make sure they were the real McCoy. "Yeah, man," he said. "Yeah."

Flukey was about to get on a fast-talking roll. I could tell.

"Shit, man. That dude was all gray and shit. I wondered what did him in. My uncle just got back from Vietnam. He saw stuff like that all the time. Wait till I tell him. Shit, man. That dude was real real dead, wasn't he? I could not be like Burk, man. I could *not* do that stuff all day. That shit's got to make you strange. I bet that's why his woman left. And the way it smells in there? Man, a dead body, dude. Square business dead. Maybe he was murdered, wouldn't that be wild? Just whacked, man, bumped off, killed, electrocuted or something."

He spat again. "Man oh man. Dude was dead sho nuff."

Shom said nothing through all of this. He didn't even gloat or call me a punk. We turned off on our street, and Flukey headed up to Labadie Ave., where he lived. Shom stopped me before we mounted the steps. "Don't tell anybody where we've been," he warned.

I snorted. "You mean where *you've* been. I haven't been anywhere."

"You know what I mean," he said.

He was quiet all evening. He hardly ate anything at dinner. At one point he looked up from his plate and glared at me. "What are you looking at?"

I hadn't been thinking about him at all. "Huh?" I said. "You must be losing your marbles."

"Shut up!" Shom shouted. "Always running your mouth! You should just shut up sometime!"

Pop was as confused as I was. "What's with you, Superstar?"

Mom came to Shom's rescue, like she always did. "You all leave him alone," she said. "He's obviously not feeling well."

Mom was right. Shom took a long bath, although that wasn't unusual. Sometimes he bathed two or three times a day, until the hot water ran out. He stayed in so long, however, that I was beginning to suspect he had drowned. Immediately I regretted that my last words to him had been mean ones. I was relieved when he finally emerged, looking thoroughly scrubbed and vaguely troubled in his red plaid robe. He went to bed early, leaving his oatmeal cookies untouched. They stayed on the kitchen table all night, still in the brown paper bag he brought them home in.

While it was strange for Shom to turn in early, I was always in a hurry to get to sleep because I got revenge in my dreams. I undid the day's disasters and rewrote them to suit my most fervent desires. I had control. Everyone listened to me, and there was no end to my handsomeness. I had a smile that broke girls' hearts and an effortless style that every boy wished was his own. I had glorious hair and a strong throwing arm and I wasn't allergic to grass and I never ever had a runny nose. I had contracts to endorse all my favorite snack foods, and every day a truck pulled up outside my mansion to deliver a fresh supply of Bub's Daddy bubble gum and Fiesta corn chips and Tahitian Treat in frosty glass bottles.

That night I had just slugged a game-winning round-tripper for the home team. I circled the bases to the roar of the adoring crowd. I slapped five with all my teammates and took a congratulatory call from the president, and still the fans stood and applauded. I stepped out from the dugout and tipped my cap to the yelling crowd. I was smiling and blowing kisses and the crowd was yelling and yelling and—

Shom was sitting up in bed and yelling his head off. I rolled over and rubbed my eyes, then clenched them tightly as light flooded the room. Shom was still shouting when Pop came rushing in, followed by Mom. Pop said, "What in the Sam Hill?"

Pop tried to shake him awake, but Shom fought him off. He panicked and struggled until Pop gradually rocked him into something close to serenity. "Hush, boy," he said gently. "Hush. Hush."

It should have been my moment. My bed, usually soaked by now, was nice and dry, and Shom's face was wet with tears.

I was cool and collected while he was a mess, his beloved curls tousled and damp, his chest heaving and breathless from all his screaming like a girl. I should have snickered in his face, but I couldn't because I knew where he had been during that terrible interval, what he'd gone through while I was circling the bases and thrilling my fans. I knew that he'd made his way back to Burk's, past the round man and down the dark hall to the gray body on the table. Somehow I also knew there'd been an endless row of tables, and an endless row of bodies, that the gray men had gotten up and gone for his eyes.

"I saw zombies," Shom said softly. "Zombies everywhere."

I should have said, "You're a punk, you know that?" Instead I moved to his bed, took his hand, and placed it firmly in both of mine. And for once I said nothing at all.

The Genius

"Teeth," she said.

Crispus stepped forward for inspection. He pulled his lips back in an exaggerated grimace, exposing his teeth and gums.

"Aah," the Grandmother commanded.

"Aah."

"You need to pay better attention to those back ones, young man."

"I will."

Placing her palm on the back of Crispus's head and pulling him close, she sniffed his neck. Detecting no odor, she seemed satisfied.

The Grandmother reached out to touch his hair but reconsidered. "Did Pristine brush and comb that before you left?"

"Yes."

His mother had in fact groomed the recalcitrant fuzz atop his head, bristling and beating each strand until it joined its fellows in precise, straight-backed majesty. But they seemed to wilt beneath the Grandmother's relentless gaze, shrinking into cowering corkscrews of impenetrable kink. The Grandmother was not impressed.

"Hmph. You sure can't tell by looking at it."

Saturdays went like this: Crispus went to D & E Fine Foods for the Grandmother while his brother Schomburg feasted on Big Mama's largesse. "Sweets for my sweet, sugar for my honey," the Grandmother would sing as she spooned a mountain of chocolate ripple ice cream into Schomburg's bowl. While Shom flexed his dimples and dug in, Crispus marched into the immaculate living room to endure his weekly ritual of humiliation, standing still and aahing on command. No matter how diligently he scrubbed and polished—sometimes until his gums bled—those molars never passed muster. It had to be some cruel trick of the genes. Schomburg could gargle mud and still blind you with his gleaming fangs.

Crispus could hear Shom in the kitchen, the dramatic sigh of satisfaction that followed each slurp, the clink of his spoon against the edge of the bowl. He summoned his courage.

"May I have some ice cream too?"

"You know as well as I do that ice cream's loaded with sugar. Sugar's bad for kids with cavities. Start brushing those back ones like you have some sense and we'll see about getting you some ice cream. Now here's my list," the Grandmother said.

Down the block from the house where Crispus lived, Pristine's brother Orville shared half of a two-family flat with Big Mama. Uncle Frank and his family occupied the upstairs half. Orville had been tutoring Roderick Bates on Saturdays. Their sessions had come about at Big Mama's suggestion, although Orville had laughed when the idea was first presented to him.

"Tutor the Genius? Big Mama, there's nothing I can teach that boy—sorry, young man."

The word *boy* was forbidden in Big Mama's house.

Big Mama snorted. "You're no slouch yourself. Roderick's teachers all tell him he's their best student since Orville Warford. Besides, he could benefit from your company. He needs some intelligent conversation."

Orville grinned. He was long and tall, with the same kind mouth as his sister, Pristine. He had been the best chemist at

Tuskegee since Carver himself, graduated at the top of his class. Inexplicably, he came home and took a job teaching high school chemistry.

"I like Roderick a lot, you know that. But he's a phenomenon, a prodigy. You show him a concept one time and you never have to mention it again. He's a steel trap."

"Then show him some different concepts, ones that he's not getting in school. Put all you've learned to meaningful use."

Orville sighed. He'd known that was coming. "Big Mama, I teach kids five days a week. I'd say that's pretty meaningful."

"They're not *our* kids."

Orville taught at a white school way out in the suburbs. It was highly unusual—perhaps unprecedented—for a black teacher to find work there, but Orville's reputation was so outstanding that the white folks had pulled strings to get him. Orville couldn't resist the state-of-the-art lab and limitless supplies. Students at the high school around the corner had been waiting for new Bunsen burners for two years. The black weekly had recently complained about the tardy equipment. "Thirteen years after *Brown*," the editorial said, "and Gateway City's schools are still separate and still unequal."

Big Mama had thrown a queen-size fit when Orville told her where he'd be working.

"What about your people?" she had demanded.

"What about science?"

For once, Big Mama had relented. Folks in the family were surprised that she hadn't given Orville more grief for coming home in the first place. She'd had high hopes for the golden one, as Frank was fond of calling him. Medical school, a doctorate in chemistry, the Nobel Prize—to hear Big Mama tell it, nothing was out of reach. But instead of blazing up into everglorious heights, Orville gathered up his awards, citations, and acceptance letters from countless graduate schools and headed back to Sullivan Avenue. He commuted daily from the same bedroom where he'd spent his exemplary youth. Big Mama told nosy neighbors that Orville was unsettled, that he had something to get straight before resuming his extraordinary ascent. More than a decade had passed and Orville was still settling, and that elusive something remained a mystery.

Orville's prize pupil was not to be found among the privileged young snots of suburbia but a mere two houses away. He had his own theories regarding the riddle of Orville's stagnation.

Roderick Bates, thirteen, was usually called the Genius, Brains, Professor, or Dilton Doiley, after the lab coat–wearing nerd from Archie comics. For all his legendary skill with solving equations, conjugating verbs, or computing faster than the cash register at Tom-Boy, he had no knowledge of his own origin. He didn't know who his father was, and his mother had made it clear that she had no interest in discussing the matter. Recently, though, he'd come across an old photo. It showed his mother beaming at her high school prom, in the bloom of beauty. Her date, tall, handsome, and devoted, was none other than Orville Warford. Accustomed to effortlessly juggling limitless columns of figures, young Roderick simply put two and two together. Over weekend discussions of quadratic equations and electrolytic solutions, Roderick watched his tutor and waited. At the end of a demonstration, Orville invariably smiled and asked, "Any questions?"

"Yeah, I got one, should be real easy for you. Are you my father?"

Every Saturday, Roderick imagined springing that one on Orville, but each week he held his tongue. He'd gladly give up everything—his intelligence, his health—to hear a man call him Son. It surprised him how much he wanted it. He was thirteen, too old for primary-grade fantasies. His mom's love, eccentric and troubled as it was, should have been enough, and he'd been blessed with greater gifts than any other kid he knew. It seemed greedy or ungrateful to want more, but there it was.

He might have gleaned some vicarious warmth from his friends' dads, but as a natural loner Roderick had few friends to claim. His peers in the neighborhood respected him for the most part, despite his solitary nature. Even the bullies—like Ira and L.B., the twin terrors of Clay Avenue—chose to issue him a free pass. Each had his own reason for going easy on the rumpled wizard in their midst. The twins, for example, had lost their mother to cancer and nourished the fantasy that the Genius would someday discover a cure. The vulgar exception to neighborhood custom was the Decatur clan, whose many dysfunctional members harbored an outsize resentment toward Roderick.

There were eight Decaturs, each meaner than the next. Even La-La, the one girl, loved to mix it up. She was the toughest kid in Crispus's fourth-grade class, a title she'd claimed by taking on Keith Wiggins. He'd given her a hard shove, which was usually enough to get kids to back down from Keith, a lanky southpaw and a charter member of the PeeWee boxing squad at Herbert Hoover Boys' Club. La-La was different, as he soon found out. She just grinned and launched a windmill-style offensive that left Keith out cold. The Decaturs had ruled the neighborhood ever since they moved onto Hebert Street about a year ago. Clever kids moved off the sidewalk and hustled to the other side of the street when they saw them coming.

But no one had warned Roderick about the Decaturs. He attended a school for gifted students in a distant community and rarely spent much time in the streets. When he finally did run into them, he was on his way home from the library, lugging a stack of books on ancient Egypt. A misunderstanding of comic proportions resulted. The bottom line, Roderick later told Crispus, is don't use *mummify* in a sentence when talking to Bumpy Decatur. He'll think you're saying something bad about his mother. The next day, when Roderick's bus pulled up to his stop at the corner of Prairie and Sullivan, the Decaturs were waiting.

Crispus had been one of a group of gawkers who watched the confrontation from the safety of Randy Pressley's backyard across the street. They peered through the knotholes in the Pressleys' privacy fence as the Decaturs stopped Roderick just a few feet beyond the front door of D & E, calmly ripped open his satchel, and began thumbing through his books and papers. Roderick took it all in stride until they came upon what looked like a diary. He broke free from Koo-Koo's grasp and lunged for it. Darwin, the second oldest Decatur, slapped Roderick with the book, so hard that he fell to the ground. La-La stepped forward and put her foot on Roderick's chest. Darwin opened the book and made a big show of preparing to read from it. What he saw enraged him. The other Decaturs looked at the exposed pages and had the same reaction. They made Roderick eat a few crumpled sheets, then ripped out the others and tossed them to the wind.

The beating was too ugly to watch. The Decaturs left nearsighted Roderick crawling blindly along the curb, the remains of his glasses crushed and scattered on the sidewalk. He muttered under his breath while trying to scoop stray diary pages from the wet trash floating in the gutter.

When he was sure that the Decaturs were long gone, Crispus crept out from Randy's yard and helped the Genius struggle to his feet. Roderick leaned against the brick exterior of D & E, huffing and puffing while Crispus dashed along Prairie, grabbing as many of the Genius's papers as he could. He couldn't help glancing at a diary entry, and found that he couldn't make out a single word.

"Tout a été réalisé," it read, "à l'exception de la façon de vivre."

"I appreciate the help," Roderick said. He had two black eyes. Crispus dragged the heavy satchel while the Genius limped home.

"What's in this satchel, bricks?"

"I'm surprised there's anything now. Those Decaturs were thorough."

"See," Crispus said. "That's something you should think about doing diffcrent."

"To what are you referring?"

"There you go again. 'Thorough.' 'Referring.' There must be easier ways to say what you mean. Go on using those big words all the time and you're just begging for someone to beat you up. It's like wearing a sign on your back."

"So I'm supposed to take advice from an eight-year-old?"

"Nine. And look at me. I'm still standing, right?"

"Touché," the Genius replied.

"Come again?"

"I mean, right on."

"Now you're talking. . . . Your papers? I couldn't read any of the words."

Roderick nodded as if it hurt to nod. "They're French—this week. It's as good as a code."

"So that no one can tell what you're writing."

Roderick smiled as if it hurt to smile. "Maybe they should call *you* the Genius."

"I guess that's what made Darwin so mad."

"I guess so."

The two youngsters reached Roderick's front stoop. Almost immediately, his porch light winked on. Crispus knew that the Genius's mysterious mom was watching from somewhere within. Roderick's back was to his house, so she couldn't have seen his two shiners.

"Thanks again," Roderick said. He tried to smile but gave up about halfway through the effort.

"Tell me something, Gen—— I mean Roderick. What does it mean? Towta eety realize—something."

Roderick frowned. "Oh, you mean 'Tout a été réalisé, à l'exception de la façon de vivre.' "

"Yeah. What does it mean?"

Roderick reached down and took his satchel from Crispus's outstretched hands.

"It means 'Everything has been figured out, except how to live.' "

After word of Roderick's pummeling had wound its way through all the houses on Sullivan Avenue, the Grandmother decided that the Genius would have permanent access to the various homesteads of the Warford clan. From here on, she instructed Ed, Schomburg, Crispus, Lorenzo, and Cassandra (Uncle Frank's kids), they were to embrace Roderick like a long-lost brother.

"Behold," Crispus's father proclaimed when he heard the edict. "The matriarch has spoken."

"Behold," said Crispus's mother, "a man who evidently plans to sleep on the couch."

Privately, Crispus was thrilled. He sensed a kindred spirit lurking beneath the brilliant misfit's disheveled exterior.

Big Mama had a talk with Roderick's mother, Gloria Bates. In all the years of Roderick's life, Big Mama was one of the few people known to meet face-to-face with Gloria. Crispus occasionally saw Gloria at the window of the house she shared with her only child, or standing just inside the front door clutching her housecoat with her thin fingers as Roderick rambled down the walk. But he couldn't remember ever seeing her set foot on the front porch.

Some folks in the neighborhood said she was crazy or on dope. Pristine, who'd known Gloria since they were skinny schoolgirls, was more sympathetic. She preferred to say that Gloria was "nervous."

Big Mama silenced any foul gossip that threatened to stain the residents of the Bates household, staring down the foolhardy with her notorious glare. The only neighbor allowed to cross the threshold, she looked in on Gloria with the loving vigilance of an overprotective mother. She sat in for Gloria at Roderick's school functions and saw that he got first dibs on Ed's and Lorenzo's hand-me-downs. From whispered confidences and heartfelt confessions, Big Mama deduced that Gloria wanted more for her exceptional son than she'd managed for herself. Taking that fervent desire to heart, she initiated the tutoring sessions with Orville as part of a grand ambitious plan.

Now when Crispus returned from running Saturday errands for the Grandmother, he often found Roderick seated at the dining room table with Orville, books and papers spread out all around them. Crispus often arranged to be sitting on the front stoop when Roderick emerged. At first they talked about baseball cards—a common passion—before eventually expanding their agenda to include just about everything and everyone. Roderick reminded Crispus of his older brother Ed, who also knew a lot about a lot of things. Like Ed, he was patient and seemed to genuinely enjoy Crispus's persistent questioning. Their fields of expertise, however, were nearly opposite. While Roderick could go on at length about French, Latin, and Spanish, or the miracle of photosynthesis, there was nothing that Ed didn't know about politics, music, or girls. Crispus's friendship with both of them convinced him that he was about as well-informed as a little kid could be. Heck, if he wasn't careful, he might turn into a genius himself.

At times Crispus marveled at Roderick's innocence and wondered how a boy—young man—could grow up in North Gateway and be so clueless about human nature. You didn't have to be Dilton Doiley to know that big words like *thorough* and *mummify* rubbed certain people the wrong way, but Roderick continued to use them, blissfully ignorant of the stares and double takes he inspired.

Then there was the Grandmother. Roderick seemed to think of her as a saint in possession of a boundless and infallible goodwill. He even confided that his mother revered Big Mama as the "truest Christian" she'd ever known. Crispus begged to differ. He thought of her as a bossy figure who sucked all the light out of any room she entered. The way she favored Schomburg even tested his mother's patience, but Pristine had club meeting on Saturdays and was never around to witness Crispus's weekly inspections. "Last year she told me that I was the only third-grader she ever met who had a problem with body odor," Crispus once told Roderick while admiring the Genius's Tom Seaver rookie card.

"No way," Roderick said.

"Yeah, way. She said if it wasn't for my bad breath to balance it out, my B.O. would drive folks to distraction. She wants Schomburg to get his own room so that I can keep my funk to myself."

"You're making this up."

"If I'm lying I'm flying. She inspects me every Saturday. Come early if you don't believe me."

$\mathcal{T}$he following Saturday, Roderick arrived ahead of schedule on some feeble pretense, just in time to see Big Mama peering into Crispus's wide-open mouth. The Grandmother didn't miss a beat.

"Hey there, sugar dumpling," she said. "Grab yourself something to drink while Orville's getting himself together. Big Mama will get you some snacks as soon as I send this one to the store."

Roderick nodded, taking it all in. He could hear Schomburg in the kitchen, slurping far more than necessary.

$\mathcal{A}$ week later, Roderick met Crispus in front of D & E and told him he had a plan.

"So what's on that weird mind of yours? The Gran——Big Mama's not going to appreciate me keeping her waiting."

"*Appreciate?*" Roderick eyed Crispus mischievously. "Wouldn't it be easier just to say *like*? Don't worry, you can blame it on me."

Roderick was holding a brown paper sack. He raised it with a flourish and waved it in front of Crispus as if it were a magic talisman.

"Got something here," he announced. "Follow me, por favor."

"Después de usted."

Crispus followed Roderick outside and around to the back of the store. They sat in the shade, facing the alley.

He pulled a pint of ice cream from his sack. Crispus recognized the purple Sealtest carton.

"Chocolate ripple, right?" Roderick brandished two flat wooden spoons and smiled.

"Fo' sho," Crispus said. He reached for the offered carton and quickly flipped it open.

"That's not all," Roderick said. He reached in the sack again and produced two small, tightly wrapped packages.

"Baseball cards," he said triumphantly. He tossed a pack to Crispus.

Crispus opened it and let out a whoop. "Man oh man! Curt Flood and Lou Brock in the same pack."

Roderick laughed. "Looks like today's your lucky day."

The two friends relaxed and enjoyed their cool treat. Crispus amused Roderick by imitating Schomburg, slurping enthusiastically and smacking his lips.

The sun overhead beamed intensely, making it warm even in the shade. Crispus examined the back of the Lou Brock card.

"All right," he said. "Tell me what you know."

Roderick closed his eyes. "Okay. Middle name is Clark. Born June 18, 1939, in El Dorado, Arkansas. Bats left, throws left. Five eleven, 170 pounds."

Crispus nodded his approval. "Good. Now what's so special about 1962?"

"Easy. First full season in the majors. Played 123 games. Struggled a bit at the plate, although an average of 263's nothing to sneeze at. And he already showed clear indication of his brilliant speed with sixteen stolen bases."

Crispus shook his head. "Man oh man. How do you have time to learn all this stuff?"

"No es nada. It's nothing. And I don't *try* to learn it, I just do. It's not like balancing equations or anything. If I see the back of the card, I can usually manage to see it again in my head."

Crispus smiled. "I guess that's why they call you the—"

"Well, looky here. If it ain't the muthafuckin' genius."

Crispus immediately recognized the voice as belonging to Bumpy Decatur. He didn't want to look up, but he had to. Into the leering faces of Bumpy and his brother Darwin.

"He ain't no genius," Darwin said. "That punk be fakin'. He don't know shit."

Roderick said nothing.

Crispus extended the purple carton. "Y'all want some ice cream?"

"Shut up, Beanshots," Bumpy said. He said it with such violence that spit flew from his mouth and just missed Crispus. "This ain't about yo' nappy-headed ass. You lucky La-La ain't here or I'd let her beat the shit outta you." He turned to Roderick.

"Stand yo' ass up when I'm talkin' to you!"

Roderick reluctantly complied.

"Everybody always goin' round talkin' 'bout you a genius. What you think? Is you one?"

Roderick sighed. "Genius is relative," he said weakly. The witty Roderick was fast disappearing. The muttering Roderick was taking over.

Darwin snorted and snarled with the confidence of a bully who has many brothers. "We ain't talkin' about yo' goddamn relatives. I'm talkin' about *yo'* sorry ass."

Bumpy laughed and shoved Roderick. "He ain't got no relatives nohow, except his crazy-ass mama. That bitch ain't nothin' but a dope fiend."

"What did you say?"

Something in Roderick's tone made Crispus look up at his friend. Muttering Roderick was gone, just like that.

"You heard me. I said that bitch ain——"

Bumpy grunted as he fell, hitting the ground before he could finish the sentence. There was a moment of silent astonishment as he rubbed his jaw and stared at Roderick, who was studying his own fist as if it belonged to someone else. Crispus rose to his feet, ready to run.

Roderick tried to explain. "Look, I—"

"Aw naw," Bumpy said. He was grinning now. "That's my game, fo' sho."

Darwin grabbed Roderick and held his arms. Bumpy moved so fast that Crispus didn't register the fact of his motion until he had pulled back, a flash of silver glinting in his hand.

Roderick slumped.

"Teach you to mess with me, bastid!" Bumpy shouted.

"C'mon, Bumps, les go!"

They took off in a flurry of footsteps.

Crispus turned to Roderick. He was slowly sliding down the wall, eyes open. His hand pressed against his shirt. Between his fingers, a trickle of blood.

"Roderick! Did he?"

"Stabbed me," Roderick gasped. "I think it was a screwdriver."

"Man oh man! What should I do?"

"Get one of those pallets over there. Elevate my feet."

Several pallets leaned against the wall next to the back door of D & E. Crispus knocked one down and dragged it over to Roderick. He lifted his friend's feet and placed them on top.

"Good," Roderick said. "Now get help."

"No way," Crispus protested. "I'm not leaving you here. Forget about it."

Roderick smiled despite his pain. His fingers were now wet and red. "I'm not going to die," he said. "I'm pretty sure he didn't get any of my internal organs."

"You sure?"

"Pretty sure."

"Pretty sure? What kind of sure is that?"

"Hey, are you doubting the Genius?"

The back door of D & E burst open. The butcher ran out in a crimson-spattered apron. "I hear you little cretins! Always loitering in back of the store. This ain't your house, so go home, why don'tcha?"

He paused, taking note of the small boy kneeling beside his stricken friend. The wet hand on the shirt. The buttons misaligned.

"Jesus God," he said. "I'll get help. I'll call the cops." He ran back inside.

"Hear that? Help is coming."

Roderick chuckled weakly. Crispus somehow knew that he should keep him talking.

"Why are you laughing? We got a serious situation here."

"I was just thinking how good it would be to see my mother right now."

"Makes sense to me," Crispus said, but Roderick didn't hear him.

"It's funny," he said. "All my life I've wished and wished for a father. And now I can't think about anything else but my mama."

He closed his eyes. "Do you hear me, Mother? Le necesito, mama."

The Genius continued to laugh. The blood continued to ooze. Slowly and thickly, like chocolate ripple melting in the sun.

Sic Transit Gloria

*R*oderick's voice was the third sign.

All these years of fearing—maybe even believing—that I've been marked by the Devil. All these years spending every living minute looking over my shoulder for Satan, and here come God, right on time.

There's no stories on Saturdays. Can't watch the Ames family on *Secret Storm*. Can't watch *General Hospital* and see if Jessie's gonna dump Dr. Brewer for good. My boy's away studying, and I'm keeping company with *Tent Meeting* on the gospel station. *Tent Meeting* with Rev. Josiah Banks. I'm a regular. When my disability comes, I always write a check to that wonderful Rev. Banks. He's going to remember me in his prayers for the sick and shut-in. I've never seen him, but I can tell by the way he sounds that he's a handsome man. And a good one too—didn't he tell me to never doubt my God? Oh yes, I know that God is real because these moving feet are a testament to His Grace.

The Swan Silvertones begin to sing "Walk with Me." I hear their harmonies fade and I turn to shake my radio. It's like someone's turned the volume down. Then I hear my son's voice ring out strong as faith.

"Do you hear me?" he says. "Do you hear me, Mother?"

The sound doesn't enter my ears like noise normally does. It's born in my bones, rises out of my pores, and takes shape in the air. It makes me hot and cold at the same time. Chills up my spine, sparks in my limbs. My son speaks, God touches me, and I get up and go. But first I have to get dressed.

I know something has happened because Roderick seldom calls me Mother. It's usually Mama, and just as often it's Madre or Ma Mère. Lots of languages in that young man.

The radio gets louder and I haven't even touched the dial. The Silvertones sing like they got the Holy Ghost. I know how they feel.

Walk with me, Lord.

My way has been rough, but I can't complain because I brought it on myself. Big Mama says don't blame God when the flesh won't function, and I'm sure she's right. Nothing holding me back but my own weak will.

Big Mama's as good to me as my blood mama was, God rest her soul. But when she loses her patience, Big Mama can't hold back. She gets to snorting and says she got to tell it like it is. She lights up a Viceroy and tells me, "Look here, Gloria, you know where the front door is and ain't nothing wrong with your feet."

I tell her it's not that easy. She says nothing ever is.

I love this song. Rev. Banks plays something by the Silvertones almost every Saturday. Let me take another look at this blouse. I'm not the best at buttoning.

Folks got tired of me saying I had to stay inside to keep the Devil out. I used to tell them, "Better mind your own doorstep and stop creeping around mine. I'm on Satan alert all day every day."

After a while they stopped coming around. Even Orville. Don't suppose he found much joy in talking to me through the screen door. If it wasn't for Big Mama and the deliveryman from Tom-Boy, it would just be Roderick and me.

When I say to Big Mama that I'm trying to raise my son to be a good man, she can't help but snort. "How's he going to be a good man when he sees you doing your best to avoid being a good woman? A good woman can hang her own clothes on the line. A good woman can meet with her son's teachers at school. A good woman can pick out her own cuts at the butcher shop." A few more *good womans* and she gets me to crying. She feels bad and prays with me, says she'll be back when I'm feeling better.

While I'm on this tedious journey,
I want you, Lord, to take a little walk with me.

Oh, those Silvertones. They know how to bring the good news. If Rev. Claude Jeter doesn't sing like an angel, I don't know who does.

Manhood's a sensitive subject with Big Mama. She's from the South. Florida. Her daddy worked in a turpentine camp. Did fine, she said, until a white man called him "boy." They locked horns, and her daddy laid that man against a blade and split him like a log. He ran from camp, but he didn't run far. Just went home and got his family together. Packed them up, gave his oldest son a rifle, and told them to head north. Big Mama was just a little girl, but she remembers. She says her mama begged and pleaded for her daddy to run, but he said he'd decided that running was for boys, and he was nobody's boy. He stayed and fought, and he died fighting. The family came up to Gateway City with little more than her daddy's pennies and the clothes on their backs. Her mama told her that folks could say many things about her father, but no one could ever say that he wasn't a man.

Big Mama grew up and met a fellow. He started calling on her, and things got serious.

Now where did I put that house shoe? Don't imagine I got an outside shoe that fits. Suppose I gave most of them to charity.

One day Big Mama goes to see him on his job. Sees him bowing and scraping but tells herself he's got no way around that. But then a white man calls him "boy" and he keeps right on scraping. Big Mama tells him her daddy couldn't rest right if she married a man who didn't know how to stand up for himself. She told him she wouldn't see him again, and she didn't. She found another fellow after a while, married him, and now she's widowed. She'll be the first to tell you they raised sons, not boys. She called them young men when they were still in the cradle and brought them up never to even say the word. Now she's got me calling Roderick a young man. Of course he is thirteen.

Rev. Banks says God can pull a blessing from a burden, and who knows that better than me? I got Roderick in my darkest hour, and look what he's become, the smartest *young man* in the neighborhood if not all of Gateway City. People call him the Genius. He didn't tell me, Big Mama did. The deliveryman brings me my groceries, right? He's heard stories, doesn't want to look me in the eyes, and that's just fine with me. One day he sees Roderick's picture on the piano, and all of a sudden he wants to be my best friend. "The Genius is your son?" he says. "How did you do it?" He doesn't want to take a tip. All of a sudden my money's no good.

The Genius, they call him. *I hear you, Son. Can you hear me?*

Orville and I were at the senior dance. My mama, rest her soul, had made me the most beautiful dress, and my corsage came straight from Big Mama's garden. Orville was headed toward Tuskegee, and I still had a year to go. I told him he had nothing to worry about. Just write me regularly, I said, and I'll wait. How about that?

That was before the dance. I don't know what got into me that night. I always had a notion that Janice Compton wanted him for her licking stick, and then I find out that she's going to Tuskegee too? Took all I had not to give her what-for in the toilet. She was hogging the mirror just as fancy as she please, primping and pulling on that hair Miss Bernice had nearly hot-combed to death. I'd've had to be blind not to notice her in Miss Bernice's all that Saturday morning, sitting in that chair with smoke coming out of her skull. Later she gets the nerve to cut in on me. "May I have this dance?" Practically stepping on my feet.

"No, you may not," I answer, but Orville looks at me like I'm from the moon. He whispers to me that it wouldn't be polite to refuse her, this being their last school dance and all. They dance and I pout. I pout and they dance.

Look at this face. It's a wonder this mirror doesn't crack. Orville used to say that my smile could launch a thousand ships. He loved the perfume I used to splash on before we went out. Soap and water will have to do today. Hope I don't scare anybody.

Walk with me, Lord.

When Orville gets ready to take me home, I tell him to go by himself. Orville says his mother will never forgive him if he lets something happen to me. I tell him that's his problem. I figure I can get a cab if I walk down to Vandeventer. It's a warm spring night and the sky is full of stars. I'd just crossed Sarah Street when the Devil dragged me off the road and took me from behind. Tore me open and left me unconscious in back of the Comet Theatre. I felt the force of his anger and his hot breath on my neck, but I never saw his face.

I didn't let Orville come see me, not in the hospital, not when I went back home. Not even before he went off to school. I was proud and covetous, and God punished me for it. Orville didn't have nothing to do with it. If he's so smart, then he knows that without me saying so.

There's that house shoe. Will Roderick mind if I'm still wearing my robe? I just have to put it on over this outfit. Maybe it will comfort him since he's seldom seen me in anything else. Even when it's hot I can't help holding it close to me, wrapping it tight to keep the Devil out. I like the feel of that familiar cloth between my fingers.

I spent nine months thinking bad thoughts—the Devil had my mind, you see—but the Lord was stronger, and He had plans beyond my understanding. See, Roderick came from God, I know that, but that doesn't make him safe from the Devil. Satan never gets tired. He just says, Okay, Lord, you won that round. The next one's mine.

I could hardly look at him when he was born. Sometimes I got to trembling with joy just looking into his sweet brown eyes. Other times—well, my mom handled him more than I did. She was always telling me that he was different, that God must have touched him. She reads him stories, says she thinks he's following along. At first I don't pay her no mind, but as he grows I can't ignore he's special. He was reading before other babies could speak, counting before their milk teeth came in. I still didn't rejoice because I was too busy looking out for the Devil. He found me once and he could find me again. I heard him sometimes, tiptoeing around my yard, fiddling with the windows in the dark of night.

My mother used to tell me every time Orville came back from school. She'd come back from Big Mama's full of talk about all the things he was learning. "Yes, ma'am, I'm majoring in chemistry. Yes, ma'am, I made the honor roll again. No, ma'am, I don't have a girlfriend yet."

Mama used to beg me to do little things. "Can't you just sit on the front porch for a little while? How about the back porch then? Can I at least tell Orville that you said hello?" I said no and stayed inside. Even when she told me that Janice Compton had run off to New York with a sharp-dressed gambler.

Orville wrote me regularly, just like he promised. His letters went unopened.

He tried to come see me when Mama died, God rest her soul. I didn't go to the funeral. Graveyard's got too many places for the Devil to hide. I convinced myself that Mama would have understood. Orville came by later and knocked and knocked. I got a good look at him through the curtains in the living room, but I didn't answer. He left me some flowers on the porch.

Big Mama promised my mother she'd look after me, and she has. She's the truest Christian I've ever known.

Jesus, hold my hand.
Come on and hold my hand.
Come on and walk with me.

God sent me the first sign when I was moving some things in the attic. A box overturned. A photo of Orville and me slid onto the floor, followed by a heap of envelopes. They had Orville's letters in them. I had never opened a single one. We posed for that photo at the dance before the troubles began. Orville looked so handsome, and I wasn't too shabby either.

That picture should have had fourteen years of dust on it, but it was clean as the day it was made.

Big Mama says Orville's been waiting all these years for me, that the picture is as pure and eternal as his love. That's why no dust can cling to it, she says. Orville hasn't exactly said as much, but Big Mama's figured it out. She tells me Orville's behavior isn't natural, that I should put the man out of his misery. I tell her it's not that easy. She says nothing ever is.

She lights up a Viceroy and says, "You so busy blaming the Devil when maybe you should be giving credit to God."

I ask her what she means, and she says the worst thing that ever happened to me gave me Roderick, the best thing that ever happened to me. I tell her that has already occurred to me, but she acts like she doesn't hear me. Big Mama's like that. "God knew what He was doing and still does," she says. "Maybe the Devil didn't have anything to do with it."

I look over my shoulder to make sure the Devil isn't listening. "Why would God hurt me in order to help me?"

I think I got her cornered, but she snorts and blows smoke. "The Lord works in mysterious ways," she says.

Later I reflected on her words, and I admitted to myself that I found some wisdom in them. Then when Roderick got beat by those awful kids—it made me sick to my stomach to see all that hurt in his sweet brown eyes—Big Mama's meaning became even clearer. At first I wanted to say that Roderick suffered at the hands of the Devil, that in a moment of weakness my watchfulness had failed. Now I know that it was God after all, giving us a way to get Roderick and Orville together. That was the second sign.

Roderick doesn't say much about his time with Orville, but I've noticed the way he looks forward to it. Big Mama says it does Orville a heap of good to talk science with a young colored man for a change. She says Orville looks renewed after meeting with my son. And Roderick's steady blooming, like the flowers in Big Mama's yard.

Oh, the song is ending. Time to rise up like Lazarus and leave my cave. Lord, You have given me signs. Now I am asking You for strength.

I feel You, Lord. The Holy Spirit sparks my limbs. I have love in my heart. I have fire in my bones. I will cross this threshold. I will set foot on this porch. I will not be swayed by the brightness and confusion. I will make my way in this tedious world. My son needs me.

I will be as strong as my son's voice, strong as faith.

I love you, Son. Hold on. Mama's on her way.

You're listening to Tent Meeting *with the Lord's faithful servant Rev. Josiah Banks. You just heard the Swan Silvertones, who have testified of God's goodness— praise Him! Now it's time for the portion of our service devoted to the devout who find themselves—amen!— unable to walk with the Lord in the light of this day. We will walk for you, saints—hallelujah!—in Jesus' name.*

We send out blessings to the sick and the shut in.
Brother Coolidge, we are praying on that heart attack.
Sister Morris, we are praying on that arthritis.
Sister Joan Dear got the sugar, we remember you today.
Sister Gloria Bates, child of God, we couldn't ever forget
    about you . . .
We know that you all are looking for a healing.
We pray that each and every one will be blessed of God.

He's a healer—umm—when you need a healer.

He's a way maker—hah!—when you need to make
a way.

God said come unto me who are weary—well!—and I
will give you rest . . .

Drunk on History

*T*here was plenty of room for signs in the modern world, and few believed it as fervently as Reuben Edward Jones Sr.

As Reuben saw it, each day our lives became more crowded and confused; highways and hallways alike were so packed with people, twists, turns, and distractions that it was getting harder and harder to find the path that would take you where you needed to go. What better way to help folks navigate than a perfectly placed, beautifully painted sign? Reuben had painted them since he was a child. His first, in bold crayon, had hung above the entrance to his bedroom and warned everyone to Keep Out. It was nicely done, with cleanly executed block letters easily seen from a distance. It was also a sign that no one in his family was inclined to notice or obey. But their hardheadedness cramped neither his enthusiasm nor his style, and by high school he was first choice to design campaign posters for student council candidates, banners to be hung up in gymnasiums-turned-ballrooms, love letters skillfully rendered with pen, ink, and a steady hand.

He loved the mobility of the sign painter's life. You threw your supplies in the back of your Rambler, strapped your ladders to the roof, and away you went. It was blissful: To be up on a scaffold in the open air with the sun on your face and the wind on your back surely beat being cooped up in a building somewhere, staring at the same four walls, sharing the same stale air with a bunch of equally bored pencil pushers and paper shufflers. He realized that kind of work was still rare for black men outside the post office, and plenty of them would be happy to have it.

But not Reuben Jones. So after college he put his diploma in a bureau drawer and hung up a shingle on Gateway's North Side: Black Swan Sign Shop. He'd never get rich, but he'd never get bored either. And business was brisk. He quickly built a reputation for fairness and good work, and he had a lot of repeat customers. Every time the cost of a hot link or a haircut went up, new signs were required. Every time inventory needed to be slashed and clearance tables emptied, more signs. Every time a man died in a confrontation with police, Reuben's reliable hands were called into service. 50% Off. Try Our Fries. Teenie's Lounge. Curly's Candy. Off the Pigs.

Not that he didn't like "fine" art. To the contrary. He'd taken his bachelor's in studio art, aced his finals in drawing, painting, and sculpture. He just didn't see much purpose in pursuing a distinction between one kind of playing in paint and another. As word of his talent continued to spread, portraits became part of his bread and butter. Every self-respecting minister, he discovered, needed a dignified likeness of himself to decorate the lobby of his church. Ananias Goode was talking about sitting for him. Reuben didn't see a need to draw any lines between portraits and posters, gangsters and pastors. All of them stood to benefit from a bit of carefully applied color, an elegant hint of shadow or shading to give them added dimension. If they could coexist in the world at large, who was he to grumble?

Tomorrow he'd work one of the last outside jobs of the season. He and his best friend, Lucius Monday, would stencil a couple of cabs for Marcella Taxi, then they'd head over to

Franklin and Easton to take a look at a wall. There was talk of a mural going up there in the spring of '68, with the men of the Black Swan handling the job.

Tonight, though, he is inside his studio. The weather is mild, and his house is quiet. Earlier, he could hear Ed through the thin wall, grunting as he lifted weights in the little corner he'd carved out of the furnace room. He pictured Ed stretched out on the weight bench they had made together from scraps of wood, straining against the iron while a trio of Mr. Universes—Sergio Oliva, Dave Draper, Frank Zane—stared down at him from the walls.

Now, flights above Reuben on the top floor, Ed, having cooled down and bathed, reclines in an old kitchen chair. He listens to Trane and rubs charcoal across his sketch pad. Working from memory, he strokes the soft jawline of Charlotte onto his paper, the cottony sweep of hair above her delicate ear, the soft curve of her lip. Down one flight of stairs, Pristine watches TV and munches pumpkin seeds while thumbing through *Jet* magazine. "The Week's Best Photos" features Huey Newton, Mahalia Jackson, and Sammy Davis Jr. A small mound of discarded shells fills the ashtray on her nightstand. In the room next to Pristine, Shom and Crisp debate the relative merits of Captain Nice and Mr. Terrific before falling asleep and dreaming, respectively, of ice cream and baseball.

The humble wooden door leading to Reuben's studio gives no hint of the uproarious jumble inside. Running along the entire length of the far wall is a homemade drafting table, spacious enough to accommodate a man carefully stenciling a price sign to hang over the cash register at Pioneer Barber Shop, or designing a pair of praying hands à la Albrecht Dürer for the pediment above Angelus Funeral Home. There is even room for a rambunctious boy or two to stand on upended milk crates and "work" beside their father when the mood suits them all. Next to the table stands a thick chunk of wood nearly four feet tall, from which a half-formed figure of a man struggles to emerge, his shoulders and torso pocked with chisel marks.

All about are brushes, maulsticks, brushes, cans of thinner. Brushes. Tubes of tempera. Acrylic. Oils. Charcoal. Brushes. A large magnifying lamp, clamped to the edge of a smaller drafting table mounted on wheels. Empty, paint-stained coffee cups from White Castle. Boxes of broken pastels, a big, comfortable, shabby chair. Brushes. Pipes, tobacco, cigar stumps in an ashtray made from pennies welded together. Price placards for Ardell's Beauty Parlor; rough sketches of the enormous pig that will hang, illuminated, above Q-King Barbecue. A half-finished portrait of Big Mama that neither artist nor subject was particularly enchanted with. Ads torn from *Ebony, Sepia, Jet*. Old signs for Pierre Record Shop, Cashmere Cleaners. Construction-paper Christmas trees, made by his kids. A fortieth birthday card from his wife. Lining the crowded windowsill, cans that once held frozen lemonade from Kroger and coffee from Maxwell House, now crammed with more brushes.

These are only some of the things that clutter Reuben's room of wonders. He sits in the middle of it all in that shabby chair, nose buried in a book he occasionally lowers to glare at the blank canvas perched on the easel, taunting him. Somewhere in that blankness lurk the innocent features of Cheryl Grimes, a young girl whose portrait he has agreed to paint. After meeting with her father, Reuben had come as close to melodrama as he ever did. "That man made me feel like painting his little girl was a matter of life and death," he had told Pristine, "for all concerned."

Muttering, he lowers the book to his lap and squints at the canvas, willing the illuminating contours—the eyes, cheekbones, the forehead, the chin—to emerge and reveal themselves. So far, nothing.

He calls his space a studio. Pristine calls it a firetrap.

Some nights, this intimate environment is where Reuben gets closest to thinking seriously about heaven, enjoying the silence, pondering life and art while all his favorite people are under his roof.

On such nights, sitting still can be as fulfilling as when the Surge seizes hold of him and he rises to its call. Soon he is happily lost, wiping away the foggy expanse of canvas to magically expose what's been hidden in it all along. Anything will give up its secrets if you love it enough, and oh, how he loves painting—especially when he's in the thick of it, his mind following the motion of his hand rather than guiding it, fingers and colors joined in a wondrous dance, dipping and twirling, daubing and dappling, again and again. It was as if the bristles disappeared and his hand became the brush. Meanwhile, the paint flowed effortlessly from somewhere deep inside him. The Surge didn't save itself for divine or elevated purposes; it could arrive while he sketched his own children or tried to capture the light of inspiration in Rev. King's eyes, but it could just as easily come when he was painting "Chitlins, Chicken, and Chops" on the side of Dempsey Wynne's Rib Hut. Nothing was beneath the spirit of Art.

He was content to bathe in this sweet, mysterious energy; he had been fortunate to know it before he even knew what painting was. He felt no need to explore its origins or to give it a human face. He'd leave the cosmic questions to Pristine. He knew she felt the same Surge when she stood and swayed in church or pressed her fingers to the soil while tending her flower beds. He knew Rose Whittier, so mousy and unsmiling on those rare occasions when her crazy husband let her leave the house, felt it when she opened her lovely lips and let all that raucous glory out; he knew Talk Much had at least some of it inside him when his mumbling changed from something vaguely disturbing to something vaguely melodious; he knew Lucius felt it when he painted, lost it when he stopped, and spent many restless hours of each day looking for it in the bottom of a bottle of Rosie O'Grady. Heaven is more than just a notion on such nights.

Tonight, stillness won't do. Tonight he needs the Surge. In the stubborn recesses of his memory, the young girl's smile hovers, teasingly indistinct.

On evenings when the Surge didn't visit his home studio, Reuben took comfort in the barely controlled chaos of his surroundings. With the furnace roaring in the other room and all the other noises of the house stilled, he could pretend he was a prehistoric man, one of the first to apply pigment to the yielding dusty rock of his cave, scratching out crude outlines of mastodons and arrows. Or he could be Scipio Moorhead in the eighteenth century, preserving Phillis Wheatley's ebony profile for the ages. Henry Tanner taking the measure of Paris, Horace Pippin doing his thing in Pennsylvania.

He'd imitated those men on the way to finding his own style. He all but prayed to them now: Pippin, guide my hand. Tanner, give me some of that grace. Above all, help me find those pictures. Sigh.

He pulls out his handkerchief, holds it to his nose and blows. His bad foot throbs. His tooth aches and his scalp itches. All of these minor maladies, he is sure, will improve as soon as he finds those photos.

Tanner's art and supplies had been tossed on the street in Philly; his classmates called him a nigger. Still he painted. So why was he, Reuben Jones, splendidly alone and free from such insults, staring at a blank canvas?

He supposed he could get up and go through his things again, turn everything over until those pictures popped out. But first he'd have to put down his battered, well-thumbed copy of *Notable Negroes,* a gift from his sister and the best book he'd ever read. Summoning his resolve, he lifts it from his lap and places it on the table.

On more than one occasion, Pristine had come down in the middle of the night and found him asleep, snoring, with the book still clasped tightly in his hands.

"Look at you, Reuben Jones," she'd say while shaking him awake. "I do believe you're drunk on history."

It was true. He couldn't get enough of the book. He couldn't believe how much stuff in *Notable Negroes* had never come up in school, and he'd gone to a historically black college. The thick volume had been shiny and leather-bound when he first unwrapped it, but over time it had been reduced to a barely-held-together, paint-splattered mess. Reuben consulted it the same way some folks turned to the Bible. He'd even named his kids from it. The last two, that is. Ed, whose formal name was Reuben Edward Jones Jr., had been born before the book entered his father's life.

Ed said he considered himself lucky. His brothers said he was just jealous.

"I would never have let Feather give that to you if I had known it would keep you up nights." Pristine was only pretending to be angry, and Reuben knew it.

"I wasn't up," Reuben would say, rubbing his eyes. "I was sleeping good until you shook me so hard. Next time, try a kiss."

Reuben had memorized large chunks of *Notable Negroes,* a handy trick for settling arguments over checkerboards and in barbershops. He grew fond of boring his buddies at the sign shop with long, heartfelt recitations about such "accomplished historical figures" as Dred Scott, Benjamin Banneker, and Ida B. Wells, and boasting about his kids' famous namesakes. The men of the Black Swan groaned each time an unwitting newcomer asked Reuben how that good-looking, ball-playing kid of his got saddled with a name like Schomburg. "He's named after an important someone," Reuben would reply. His buddies knew the rest by heart.

"As in

SCHOMBURG, ARTURO ALFONSO. Bibliographic genius born in 1874 in Saint Thomas, Virgin Islands. Raised in Puerto Rico. In 1891 he moved to New York, where he became deeply involved in American Negro culture. Eventually built a collection of more than ten thousand books, manuscripts, prints, and pieces of memorabilia that document the history and achievements of colored people. Sold his private collection to the Carnegie Corporation, which gave it to the New York Public Library in 1926.

"His poor, poor wife" was all Pristine said whenever Reuben read aloud from that passage, which he did every January 24, when he forced his whole family to celebrate Arturo Schomburg's birthday.

Pristine would sigh while slicing the cake. "I can't imagine how she put up with so much stuff," she'd say. "There couldn't have been any room for furniture, much less children."

"*Wives,* not wife" was Reuben's regular reply. "The man was married three times and fathered seven children. Too much genius for one woman, I guess."

"Rest assured, Reuben," Pristine would say. "That's a problem you'll never have to deal with."

And if anyone who walked into the Black Swan was foolish enough to wonder out loud about the origins of Crispus Jones's name, the entire sign shop responded in a chorus of righteous indignation:

ATTUCKS, CRISPUS. Born 1723, runaway slave and seaman. First American killed by British soldiers during the Boston Massacre, March 5, 1770.

Reuben's youngest son was probably the only Crispus in America, maybe even the only one so burdened since that Notable Negro went to his glory nearly two centuries ago. It was an unusual name, Reuben was always quick to acknowledge, but not so much different from Limoka, Kozetta, and Tres Bien, to name just a few of his son's classmates.

Reuben tears his eyes from the table, resisting the book's pull. The photos of the Grimes girl have to be in here somewhere. He turns slowly, taking it all in. Opposite the drafting table, bookcases spill over with cheap pulps, secondhand hardcovers, and stacks of magazines: *Popular Mechanics. Up from Slavery. National Geographic. The Souls of Black Folk.* David Walker's *Appeal.* Editions of Gateway's ambitious black papers, the *Citizen,* the *Argus,* and the *Sentinel.* And a local scandal rag called *The Evening Whirl.* More things he hadn't read in school.

In a distant corner sits a rickety record player in an equally unsteady console, its legs weathered, ragged, and bearing signs of water damage. Against one leg, a stack of albums: Billy Eckstine, Jesse Belvin, Erroll Garner. Beside it, a sketch pad belonging to Crispus and stumps of his crayons crammed in an old Dutch Master box. Where were the pictures when he'd last seen them?

Reuben couldn't remember where he knew Grimes from when he first showed up at the Swan earlier that autumn, but he knew he'd seen him before. A tall, brown-skinned man around Reuben's age, he looked kind of nervous when he entered, as if a little surprised to find himself there. Reuben and Ed were alone in the shop, a fact he guessed Grimes had already determined. He instinctively knew that Grimes was the kind of man who quickly figured out all the angles as soon as he entered a situation: the points of exit and entry, the shadows where danger could hide, the corners where prey could be mercilessly pinned down.

Grimes had hard, unblinking eyes. He looked at you as if he hated you, even if he was saying something as simple as "Hey" or "Good morning." He said both when Reuben greeted him.

"My wife and I—"

Reuben waited while the man struggled with himself.

"My wife and I . . . lost our daughter. Cheryl."

"I'm sorry to hear that," Reuben said.

"Leukemia," said Grimes, with such force and venom that it took Reuben a moment to realize that he wasn't shouting, had never raised his voice. "Twelve years old."

The man went on to say that he'd heard about Reuben's portraits and wanted one of his daughter. Reuben agreed to take on the assignment and told Grimes his price. "I'll take care of you," Grimes said.

He carefully pulled a business-size envelope out of his pocket and spread the contents on Reuben's counter. Four snapshots of a girl. Cute, grinning, tragic. Just four shots, and not very good ones at that.

Reuben studied them. "She's beautiful," he said. "Are these all you can share?"

"They're all I have in this world," Grimes replied. "We weren't much on picture taking. Not then."

Reuben realized he'd never gotten the man's name. Nor had the man ever asked for his.

"I'm Reuben Jones, by the way, and that's my son over there."

"I know."

"I'm sorry, I didn't get your name."

The man looked at Reuben a long moment, as if to determine if he was being teased. "It's Grimes," he said.

How could they have just a handful of photos of their only child? He and Pristine had at least a hundred photos for every year of every child's life. Instamatic and Polaroid, black-and-white and, frequently now, color. If they should ever lose a child—God forbid—you'd best believe they would have more than memories to go by.

He'd lost two siblings growing up and didn't have a picture of either. Pristine vowed that would never happen in her family, and when she wasn't snapping candids herself with her trusty Instamatic, she was lugging her scrubbed and Vaselined sons to Sears, where a professional photographer froze them on film at every stage of their young lives.

Pristine was fond of saying that she collected memories. She'd pestered Reuben's mom for photos of him as a boy, but his family had been far too poor to have many of those. She'd done better by their college days, keeping dozens that Reuben had barely been aware of. Pristine had shots of him in his crimson and crème tracksuit, clearing hurdles at the Jefferson Invitational, dressed up in tux and turban, holding his lantern aloft as he crossed the burning sands with his frat brothers.

At her urging, Reuben had also drawn large pastel portraits of each of their boys. They hung above the couch in the living room, a trio of smiling faces done in a style that no department-store shutterbug could ever dream of matching.

Shom and Crisp were still young and innocent enough to grin broadly for the camera. As for Ed, "going through changes" was Pristine's nice way of describing his behavior, although Reuben tended to view his son's growing rebelliousness in far harsher terms. The boy—sorry, young man—had made a scene at the last Sears session, refusing to so much as smile even slightly. Pristine grew tired of arguing and gave in, with the result being a large scowling portrait that now sat glowering on top of the piano.

"If I say Manet, he says Matisse," Reuben had complained to Pristine. "I say Harvard, he says Howard. Think I talked to my old man like that? Obviously not, since I'm still breathing. Sometimes I'm sure he's being contrary for contrary's sake and I want to get a strap and wear him out. He has no idea how many times his mama has come between me and his hide."

Ed is a hardworking fellow, I can't dispute that, Reuben thinks while sifting through the contents of a Horack's Dairy sack stuffed with papers. He still pulls down excellent grades while working long hours at SuperMart. The rest of his time, however, which used to be spent helping his mom in her garden, playing with his little brothers, or down here painting with me, now goes to talking to that girl, either in person or on my phone. I tell him to be careful with her—Charlotte's her name, I think—and he rolls his eyes and looks at me like I'm insane.

Reuben gives up on the dairy sack. He slips his shoe off and rubs his foot. He replaces the shoe and turns to a battered briefcase he occasionally carries when meeting new customers. He has offered to buy Ed a new briefcase to carry on his interviews with Ivy League alumni, but so far his eldest son has failed to muster any enthusiasm. He actually had the gumption to tell Reuben that carrying a briefcase was "jive."

Reuben thinks he knows what Pristine means when she

wishes they could stay small forever. Then he recalls the look in Detective Grimes's eyes. His Cheryl would stay young. She'd never sass her mama again, never grow up to regret it. She'd never pose with her giddy girlfriends after graduation, their mortarboards cockily askew and their eyes brimming with excitement. She'd never produce grandchildren to give her parents comfort in their old age. Her last expression, her final words, would be those of a small girl.

Reuben pictures her like Curly, asleep in her coffin. He imagines her parents bargaining with God, offering to relinquish everything to give their daughter a chance to grow old.

The briefcase yields paint sticks, swatches, an ancient painter's cap, and assorted folders, but no photos.

One day Shom and Crisp will get a little dirt above their lips and a disrespectful attitude to go with it. Crisp is just a wisp of a thing, afraid of his shadow. But too soon his voice will grow husky and he'll get to smelling himself just like Ed.

Little Crisp is the only child they'd ever come close to losing—twice. First he didn't want to come out of the womb, or so it seemed until they discovered his umbilical cord wrapped around his neck. Four years after that adventure, he nearly drowned in the lake in Fairgrounds Park.

Reuben and his two youngest had gone fishing. He and Shom had rested their poles and were tossing a ball back and forth in the grassy area a few yards from the dock. They'd brought gloves along to warm up Shom's arm for his game that evening. Crisp, ever the daydreamer, wandered right into the lake with his pole.

Reuben dived in and tugged him to shore. "Funny thing is," he later told Pristine, "as scared as Crisp is, he never even yelled. If not for the splash, I'd never have known he'd gone under. Afraid to go down the basement by himself but not afraid of the deep. That boy's a mystery."

Reuben reached Crisp in a couple of agonizing strokes, long enough for him to imagine going home without his youngest son, telling his mother he'd left him at the bottom of a lake, anticipating how it would feel to have a hole in his heart that could never be mended.

I don't really know what Grimes felt when his daughter passed away, but I have an idea, Reuben thinks, and I want to give him the opposite of that. What I felt when I held my boy in my arms, my living, breathing boy—that's the feeling I need to convey in Cheryl's portrait. Maybe I can depict some of the joy she must have brought to her father when she smiled, when he held her. I have to do that much for him.

He goes to his window and stares out at the cold street, sees the blades of grass on his lawn appear to shiver in the night wind. His mind wanders to imminent winter, which he'll spend doing inside work, touching up the lobby of the North Side Y, repainting the ceiling of the Riviera Club, and dedicating himself to portraits of Cheryl and, if he's lucky, Ananias Goode. The men of the Black Swan will be glad to get away from the Hawk, but Reuben has never minded its presence. He's not really aware of the cold once he gets in the thick of things. Even during times when he can see his breath, he starts out with just a jacket and often has to peel it off.

A jacket!

Reuben leaves his office and tiptoes up the stairs. Quietly, he enters his bedroom. Pristine has fallen asleep. On the black-and-white TV, Ed McMahon guffaws while Johnny Carson smirks. Reuben reaches in his closet and retrieves the suit jacket he was wearing when he met Grimes. Normally he wears a windbreaker, but that day he'd gone to city hall to see about a permit. The jacket's inside pocket holds what he's been looking for all night. He grabs the photos and gestures in silent jubilation. Great Kooga Mooga! He wants to click his heels, but there's not enough room and he doesn't want to wake his wife.

Adrenaline fills him as he skips back down to his studio. He lays the photos on the drafting table, grabs his private stash of black crayons. He removes the canvas from his easel and replaces it with a large sheet of paper. He feels a sketching spree coming on. Later the sketches will provide the basis of Cheryl's full-scale portrait. This calls for some music, he thinks, with the volume turned down quite low, of course. He drops the needle on the vinyl, and Erroll Garner's genius warms the cluttered space. The sun will be up soon, and cool, brittle air will greet him when he warms up the Rambler and prepares to pick up Lucius. He should get some rest before all that, but it will have to wait. A Surge is coming on.

The Boy on the Couch

*A*s soon as I decided to have a crush on Polly she had to go and change my mind. Shom said it's just as well because fat girls ain't worth a pretty boy's time. Of course he was talking about himself, not me. He said he wouldn't give the time of day to her even if she had been as fine as Diahann Carroll because he could never trust a black girl named Polly. This from a black boy named Schomburg.

Ed was keeping company with a cutie named Charlotte. Shom practically had his own fan club and was using the summer to take a break from all the adoration. He said he could barely perform his duties as line monitor during the school year because he was so busy beating off girls with a stick. Otherwise, he said, they'd rip his clothes off.

I figured it was my turn. I'd had a couple of crushes during the school year. I worshipped Linda McCulley every time she went to the blackboard and wrote a sentence in her flawless hand, her pigtails neatly braided and elegantly wrapped in ribbons. I also liked Linda Bowie, a demure beauty with long lashes and huge liquid eyes. The two Lindas were the kind of girls all the losers loved. They were the kind of girls who giggled and waved at Shom, blowing kisses to him while he stood on the corner and pretended to be a patrol boy. They were the type of girls who didn't even see boys like me. I knew I had to set my sights on a kinder, gentler target.

That's how Polly Garnett entered the picture. Our moms knew each other from the downtown department store where they both worked part-time. Mrs. Garnett had suffered a "personal crisis," and my mother was helping her get back on her feet by training her to be an Avon lady. For several afternoons they met over coffee and discussed the wonders of Skin So Soft moisturizing bath oil and the staying power of Sweet Honesty perfume. My job, enthusiastically accepted, was to entertain Polly.

The first day I took her down to the basement playroom, where we kept most of our toys. A lot of my playthings looked broken-in and worn-out—played with, that is. Shom's toys and games still had all their pieces and were arrayed as neatly as a shop-window display. Maybe that's why Polly kept reaching for things that belonged to him.

I had to tell her that the Hands Down game was, unfortunately, hands off. Same with the Johnny Speed remote-control Jaguar, the Creepy Crawlers set, and the Secret Sam attaché. I told her not to even think about putting her hands on Shom's Johnny Seven One Man Army. Its seven deadly weapons included a grenade, an antitank rocket, and an armor-piercing shell, all of which had been field-tested on yours truly. I could tell that Polly was getting frustrated.

"How about this Whee-lo?"

"Yeah, that's mine, but the wheel's missing."

We finally settled on the Avalanche game I'd received last Christmas. We set up to play in the front hallway, where our moms could keep an eye on us from the kitchen.

I knew right away that the arrangement wouldn't last long because Polly's marbles kept rolling into the living room. I could see Mom trying to ignore her while nibbling at the lemon pie Mrs. Garnett had brought with her and listening politely to her complaints. Polly's mother dabbed her eyes and asked if

Avon made a shampoo that would make a high-yellow heifer's hair fall out.

"That's all he wants with her, you know," Mrs. Garnett said, "that hair."

While her mother wept softly, Polly kept chasing marbles across Mom's just-buffed living room floor. She stayed in there a little longer each time. After the third or fourth time, I peeped in to see what was keeping her. She had the marbles in her hand and was staring at the couch. Finally she returned.

"Careful," I warned her. "My mom normally doesn't allow kids in the living room. She's got a thing about that floor in there."

After the fifth time, my mom had taken all she could stand. She made us a couple cups of Bosco, handed us a big bowl of dry cereal, and shoved us out the door.

A few minutes later Shom came rushing onto the front porch, screen door slamming shut behind him. He pushed between us like he was late for an important appointment. I wasn't studying him. He was acting all grown because Pop had finally decided he could walk down to Pierre Records and pick out his own 45. I heard him tell Petey that he was going to get "Soul Man" by Sam & Dave, but I knew that wouldn't stop him from strutting around the store and trying to examine every record they had, a crisply folded dollar bill burning a hole in his pocket. Ed never went to Pierre. He said he preferred Black Circle on Grand Ave. because they had a bigger selection and even knew something about jazz, his latest obsession. Lately he'd switched his loyalty from the Temptations and Impressions to Miles Davis and John Coltrane. Shom didn't care anything about jazz, and Black Circle was much too far away. He started whistling "Soul Man" and headed off toward Vandeventer Ave.

I had my own record collection and was thinking about mentioning that to Polly. I feared she might get distracted by Shom's dimples and loose curls. Not that Shom cared. From our parents' bedroom window, he'd watched Polly and her mom arrive. He said he thought she looked like Riff Raff on *Underdog,* only rounder.

My mom bought me a whole set of 45s from the department store where she worked. I had "Humpty Dumpty," "Jack & Jill," and a lot of other good songs. I had an album too, *Let's Play School* with Miss Kay. She posed on the album's jacket with her friend, a puppet named Mr. Owl. Miss Kay was blond and cheerful and looked nothing like the teachers at Farragut Elementary—not even the white one, Miss Gordon, who was neither blond nor cheerful.

Thinking about Miss Kay gave me an idea. I turned to Polly. "You want to play rock school?"

She shook her head. "Naw, we shouldn't exercise so soon after we eat."

Exercise? I looked at her. To play rock school all we had to do was scoot up and down the steps.

"Besides," she added, "there's still some cereal left."

I started to say that there was nothing but crumbs left, but she'd already lifted the bowl and forced her whole face into it. She put the bowl down and grinned. Bits of cereal and sugar twinkled in her eyebrows, on her cheeks, and between her teeth.

"I just love Crispy Critters," she said. "Don't you?"

"They're okay," I replied.

"Really? I figured you'd love 'em."

"Why did you figure that?"

"Because they sound like your name, Silly. How'd you get a name like Crispus?"

"My daddy gave it to me."

"My daddy got a girlfriend now," Polly said. "She don't look nothin' like my mama."

Even at nine I knew enough to change the subject.

"So," I said, "which do you like better, Quisp or Quake?"

She answered without hesitation. "Quake."

I couldn't believe it. "Me too," I said.

I was thrilled. Everybody else I knew preferred Quisp, that stupid alien with the propeller on his head.

"My mama said I could send off for Quake's cavern helmet," I boasted.

Polly looked skeptical. "Do you think that light on it really works?"

"Of course," I said. She even knew about the helmet.

"Mama's taking me to see *Doctor Dolittle*," she said. "Maybe you could come."

"Okay, if my mom says I can."

That sealed it. Love was in the air.

Long after the Garnetts left, Shom and I scooped the remains of the lemon pie from the pan and licked our fingers. It was incredibly good. Shom said something had to be wrong with her.

"Wrong with who?"

"You know who I mean. Sweet Polly Purefat."

Dimples gets one stupid 45 and thinks he can go around saying anything. I was ready to hit him. Instead I asked him what he meant.

"Why else would a ten-year-old girl, even a fat one, hang out with a bigheaded, redheaded monkey?"

I had visions of opening my bedroom window and sending "Soul Man" whizzing into the night like a flying saucer.

The next time they came over, Mrs. Garnett brought another lemon pie. I caught a whiff of her as she entered the kitchen, and she smelled delicious, just like the pie. She was wasting her time with Avon perfume. If she could bottle that stuff, she'd be a millionaire.

My mom didn't take any chances the second time. She sent Polly and me to the porch right away, fortified with pumpkin seeds and Tang. I was feeling so good about Polly that I showed her my autographed photo of Captain Nice. She had a ball and some jacks, but there was no way I was going to mess with those on my front porch in broad daylight. No telling who might pass by and see me, Choo-Choo, Petey, or even worse, one of the Decaturs. They were still on the prowl, and Bumpy being in reform school seemed to have made them even meaner than before.

I watched Polly crunch the seeds without even bothering to shell them, blissfully smacking away while salt and white stuff from the shells stained her lips.

Sure, she was a bit strange, but probably because her family was going through a "personal crisis." I still thought she was cute, despite Shom's insults. We had possibilities. We could have been real good together. I could see—and smell—a future full of lemon pies. But then she ruined everything by popping the question that would keep me up nights.

"Do he talk?"

"Huh?"

"The boy on the couch."

"What boy?"

"That white boy all the time sitting on your couch. Do he ever say anything? He always look so sad."

I watched Polly lick her lips. Could Shom be right?

"Sometimes he takes a deep breath, and lets it out. Like this." Polly gave a dramatic demonstration.

"That's called sighing," I said. "Polly, we don't have any white people in our house."

"That's what you think. There's a little white boy, he's about five or six and he's wearing old-time clothes. I saw him last time when I was chasing those marbles. I tried to say hi, but he wouldn't speak to me. I figured he was quiet because he didn't know me. Some kids ain't allowed to talk to strangers."

"Slow down. We don't have any white boy in our house."

Polly stood up and brushed off her lap. "Come on, Crispy Critter. I'll show you."

We went in.

"See," Polly said. She looked real satisfied, like she'd just beaten me at Avalanche.

I looked, but I didn't see a thing.

"No, I don't see," I told her.

Polly put her hands on her hips. "You mean to tell me that you don't see that white boy sitting right there on your couch?"

I shook my head. "What's he look like?"

Polly squinted and tilted her head. "Well, his hair's kinda long, like a girl's. He's wearing a hat. He's got a vest on, knickers, long brown socks, and lace-up boots."

I stared at the empty couch. I stared at Polly.

"You still don't see him, do you?"

Something about Polly's certainty shook me. "You're just messing with me," I said. "Why are you messing with me? Let's get out of my mother's living room before she gets mad." I turned to go.

Polly put up her hand. "Hold it. Didn't you hear that? He just sighed. Sounds awful, like he just wants to lay down and die. What's the matter, little fellow? You want some pumpkin seeds?" She approached the couch.

I approached the door. But I never took my eyes off my almost-girlfriend.

Polly turned and looked at me. "Crispus, give this boy some seeds."

"Stop teasing, Polly. Let's go."

She was pretty fast for such a round girl. Strong too. Before I knew it, she had grabbed my hand and dragged me over to the couch. I didn't see any boy, but what I did see gave me chills: There was an indentation in the seat cushion as if the material were being pushed down by something about the size and width of, say, a six-year-old. But there was no one sitting there. I began to feel the way I felt every time Shom hauled me past Burk's Funeral Home. Not good at all.

I didn't say anything, but Polly could tell that my viewpoint had changed. She touched my arm as if she hoped to comfort me. "Maybe he came with the couch," she said.

In the days that followed, I avoided the couch. I avoided Schomburg too, because I didn't want to hear his mouth. I decided to consult the best-known brain in the neighborhood: Roderick's. He was doing well since Bumpy Decatur tried to take him out with a sharpened screwdriver, real well in fact. He stood up straight these days, and I couldn't remember the last time I'd heard him mutter. His mom was doing well too.

The Grandmother loves to tell the story about Uncle Orville waiting for his star pupil to show up for his tutoring session. He's standing in the living room going on about this and that when suddenly he pauses. He rushes to the blinds and peers out the window.

"Gracious," he says.

The Grandmother says he was almost trembling.

"What is it, Orville? What do you see?"

"Big Mama," he says without turning around, "I think I've seen an angel."

Just then the phone rang. It was Mrs. Collins, our next-door neighbor. "I got the phone to my ear, but I'm watching Orville open the front door and go out on the porch," the Grandmother will recall to anyone who shows the slightest interest. "Mrs. Collins says 'Harriett, you won't believe this unless you see it with your own eyes. Quick, look out the window.' "

By then, folks up and down the block were finding any old excuse to lean out a window or fiddle with the flowers in the front lawn or take something to the car. The Grandmother chose the window, just in time to get a glimpse of Roderick's mother walking slowly but steadily up Sullivan Ave., fussing with her hair with one hand and holding her robe closed with the other. "Thus passes Glory," the Grandmother swears she heard Uncle Orville say, although now he says he can't remember saying anything.

Behind the store, the Genius had just been stabbed and I was still trying to keep him talking. All he would say was, "She's coming. She's on her way."

Sure enough, we both looked up and saw her, Miss Bates moving toward us like she was in a trance. Over her shoulder I could see Uncle Orville following behind her. His face looked like Charlton Heston's in *The Ten Commandments,* when he comes down the mountain after talking with God.

Uncle Orville and Miss Bates have been keeping company ever since. The Grandmother says it just goes to show that good love is worth waiting on. I was planning to avoid all that waiting. That's why I made plans for Polly. Looking back, I see now that I made my move too soon.

"Roderick, you believe in ghosts?"

Normally, the Genius could answer any question before it finished coming out of your mouth. This one he acted like he didn't want to tackle at all. "This is all I'll say," he said, sucking on his spoon. I had brought along a little chocolate ripple to get his brain juices flowing.

"My mother believes in spirits. And I believe in my mother."

"I don't get it," I said. I wanted one of those short, confident declarations along the lines of "Yes, the square root of four is two." Roderick could be counted on for those. Not this time.

"I don't want to say that there's no such thing as ghosts," he said, "even though I've never seen one. Until recently, I had never seen a miracle either. But I knew they were possible. In the end, Crispus, anything's possible."

Definitely not what I wanted to hear.

Maybe Ed would be more help. I had to catch him at ground level because there was no way I was going all the way up to his room on the third floor. I never liked it up there anyway and really hated it after Ed painted a giant skull on his wall. He had copied it from an album cover, a huge, leering death's-head with Day-Glo daisies on it. The mural reflected another of the many changes in Ed that made my mother suck her teeth and roll her eyes. He was getting more political all the time. Books about Karl Marx, Chairman Mao, and Che Guevara sat on his shelf, right next to his beloved Doc Savage paperbacks. I just watched and waited for the day when Ed announced that Doc Savage was counterrevolutionary and tossed those books in the garbage. That's when I would swoop in and silently scoop them up.

I hardly saw Ed anymore, between his job at SuperMart and his thing with Charlotte. To make matters worse, he and my dad weren't getting along. Ed was a top student, and my dad wanted him to shoot for Harvard or Yale. Ed told Pop that

if Jefferson U. was good enough for him then he should be able
to go there too, instead of making himself all uptight at a racist
institution. When Ed started preaching about the evils of sys-
tematic racism, Pop always cut him off.

"Get that bass out of your voice," he'd say. "You think you're
telling me something I don't know? Please. Your grandma likes
to say that there are no boys under this roof, but I'll tell you
this: there's only one man and he ain't you."

Before he found work at SuperMart, Ed used to stay up late
Friday nights watching monster movies. He was the household
authority on zombies, mummies, vampires, and all things
supernatural—not that he had much competition.

Ed disappointed me too. All he wanted to talk about was
Charlotte. He showed me her picture, and I readily agreed that
she was plenty cute. But that wasn't exuberant enough for Ed.
As far as he was concerned, she was breathtaking, phenomenal, extraordinary. Ed was big on adjectives and hadn't met any
that he had no use for. You came away from even the briefest of
conversations with him with a clear understanding of his likes
and dislikes. Incredible Coltrane. Marvelous Miles. Amazing
Spider-Man.

I gave in and decided to ask my mom where we'd gotten the
couch. She told me we got it from Nana, my dad's mom. Nana
used to be a maid for some rich white folks who used to give
her things from time to time. When my parents got married,
she gave them the couch. Mom told me all this while trying to
make one of Mrs. Garnett's lemon pies. She hoped to bring one
to the Grandmother's upcoming birthday celebration.

"Since when do you have an interest in furniture, young
man?" she asked while spooning sugar into a mixing bowl.

"Just curious," I said.

It was beginning to make sense. Those white folks must

have had a son who died on that couch. Now his spirit was trapped in it.

I shared my theory with Polly the next time she came over, but she topped me, to my considerable horror. "Maybe he didn't come with the couch," she said. "Maybe he came with the *house*."

The sensation in my bladder reminded me of that part in *The Brave Little Tailor* where he squeezes the cheese and all that liquid leaks out. I had similar feelings whenever I was scared enough to lose my natural mind. Like right then, for instance.

Polly was looking at me funny. "What's the matter with you?" she asked.

"Y-you think he came with the house?"

Polly was maddeningly calm. "Could be. If he came with the house, he probably wanders all over it. He probably just sits on the couch when he's tired, poor thing."

"Poor thing?" I was practically shouting. "Poor thing? That's easy for you to say. You don't have to live here! Bathroom! Be back!"

I ran upstairs and relieved myself. Then I went to my room, sat on my bed, and considered the situation. I didn't like to visit the third floor because it was scary up there. I didn't like to go to the basement by myself because it was scary down there. I had been avoiding the couch for several days because of the scary dents in the cushion. I was running out of places to cower.

I calmed down a lot when Polly left. It occurred to me that she may have been having fun at my expense—you know, playing a harmless joke on a stupid little nine-year-old. I entertained the possibility that Shom had told her of my scaredy-cat ways and my easily exploited fear of Burk's Funeral Home.

I convinced myself that was the case. My heart was broken, naturally. Hadn't Curly told me that women were nothing but trouble? I was forced to deal with the consequences of my failed romance when Mom gave up trying to perfect the lemon pie recipe and asked Mrs. Garnett to bring one over on the day of the Grandmother's birthday celebration. She arrived just before dark with Polly in tow.

When Polly smiled at me and said hello, I nearly growled at her. "How could you?" I said. I coolly exited, while all three women stared at me in open puzzlement. I ignored them and began to hum Etta James as loudly as I could.

I had nearly forgotten about the boy on the couch amid the hubbub at the Grandmother's house. She was enjoying her moment in the spotlight so much that she hadn't humiliated me even once. I was having a good time too, until my mother realized she'd forgotten her camera and ordered me to go home and retrieve it.

Immediately, my bladder began to bother me. "Umm, isn't the door locked?"

My mother shook her head. "No. The door is closed but the latch is off. Just make sure you pull the door shut when you leave."

I tried another tactic. "But the streetlight in front of our house is out."

Once again, Mom was undeterred. "Mr. and Mrs. Collins are on their porch. They'll look out for you."

She was right. I knew they would. Still, I was resourceful. I gathered my forces for one last effort. "Can't Ed bring it when he comes?"

Ed was working that night and would be coming late.

"Young man, you're trying my patience," Mom snapped. "Ed might have to work overtime for all we know. Get up off your hind part and get my camera. Now!"

Shot down for the third time.

It got bad for me as soon as I climbed out of the shadows surrounding our house and set foot on the porch. I thought I heard someone moving inside.

I pushed the door open just as some whispering subsided. I was certain. Maybe the white boy had invited over a few friends. "Anybody here?" I shouted, hoping against hope. "It's just me, Crispus!"

Silence. I purposely turned away from the living room as I advanced down the hall. No way I was looking at that couch. I went straight to the kitchen, trying to ignore a feeling of imminent doom.

A faint scurrying in the dining room. What was that? Mice? Insects? Giant winged beasts from hell? I looked frantically all over the kitchen. No camera. It had to be upstairs.

I stomped up the stairs, so as to avoid sneaking up on any creatures/robbers/ghosts that may have been skulking/stealing/relaxing up there. My bladder got heavier and heavier as I climbed. There was no getting around a pit stop. I went to the bathroom and urinated with one eye on the open door, prepared to stop in midstream, yell, and run for my life.

The camera was in my mom's bedroom on the nightstand next to an unopened pack of Belairs. I grabbed it: Mission accomplished. In my mind's eye I saw myself reentering the Grandmother's party to uproarious applause, beaming and waving while handing over Mom's Instamatic with a triumphant flourish. I swaggered down the stairs to the front door, thinking about my famous namesake and the courage we had in common. He had faced down angry Redcoats and I had strolled casually past a gho—Wait a second, didn't my famous namesake die?

In that terrible moment of recognition, I felt his eyes on me. I knew he was there in the dark living room. Sitting on the couch in his little knickers and boots, watching me and saying nothing. Slowly, carefully, I reached for the doorknob. That's when I heard it with awful, unmistakable clarity: a sigh. A big, long, loud one, full of tension and release, an exhalation so substantial that I imagined I felt a breeze. Instantly sweat bubbled up from every pore, then turned to ice when it touched the air. Tears welled up in my eyes, blinding me. My lungs tightened. I reached for the doorknob and missed. Instead I hit the bottom of the shade that covered the pane on the door. It flew all the way up, wrapping around the roller with a loud flapping sound. I got the knob with my second grab and flung open the door. I rushed onto the porch and pulled the door shut behind me. That white boy was going to have to make it through several inches of solid wood if he wanted to get his hands on me. Of course that might not be so hard, I realized, if he could *walk through walls*. I looked around for potential witnesses. The Collinses were no longer on their porch. The streetlight was still out.

I crossed my fingers, thought of Polly, and took a leap of faith. The darkness never felt so good.

A Taste of Honey

$\mathcal{E}$d was rubbing on his good-luck charm when he heard the front door open. Damn! He thought he'd locked it. He kept one long arm wrapped around Charlotte and gently touched a finger to her lips. Slowly, quietly, he craned his neck and stole a look around the corner.

"Anybody here? It's just me, Crispus!"

Charlotte wiggled a little, and Ed held her tighter. He leaned into her and whispered a gentle "Shh." They stood in the shadowy silence of the dining room, listening as Crispus headed to the kitchen. When the little interloper began to stomp up the stairs, Ed licked Charlotte's neck. She jumped and squealed, but Ed kept her clamped against him. "Be still," he cooed. "He's looking for something. He'll be gone in a minute."

"How do you know?"

"Trust me," Ed said. He rubbed Charlotte's belly, nuzzled her dark, delicious neck.

"Mmm," Charlotte murmured.

Emboldened, Ed worked his hand in circles, down to her softest spot.

Crispus descended the stairs.

Ed held Charlotte in the shadows, steadily rubbing.

Crispus looked intently at the door. He reached for the knob.

Charlotte felt herself dissolving. She sighed, in spite of herself.

After a frenzied false start, Crispus tore out the door, slammed it, and took off.

Ed listened for the sound of sneakers slapping the sidewalk. He let Charlotte go, went to the door, and pulled down the shade.

Charlotte breathed deep, then hugged herself. She turned to Ed. "You naughty boy," she teased. "You said there wouldn't be anyone else here."

"And there isn't," Ed said. "Not anymore. And you're the one who's naughty. You nearly scared my little brother out of his skin."

Charlotte looked up at Ed and batted her eyes. She put a finger between her perfect teeth and nibbled on it gently. "You're right. I'm a baaad girl."

Ed reached out and took both her hands in his. "Then I guess you'll have to be punished."

Charlotte giggled. "Lead the way," she said.

On the third floor, Ed blocked his windows with a navy bedspread. He turned to Charlotte, who was staring at his new mural. He admired Charlotte while she admired the art, a giant skull with daisies splattered across its crown. "It's from the latest Archie Shepp," he explained. *The Magic of Ju-Ju.*

Charlotte reached out and traced the skull's outline, her finger barely touching the wall. "You are some kind of talented, Ed Jones."

Ed chuckled. "Tell that to my old man. He didn't have much to say about it, except I should have asked his permission before doing anything to his walls. *His* walls."

"What's wrong with that?"

"What's wrong with it? It's my room, that's what's wrong with it."

Charlotte smiled. Those perfect teeth. "You didn't tell me you paid rent."

"I don't."

"You pay for your meals."

"That neither."

She snapped her fingers. "Then it's not your room. And it's not your house."

Ed frowned and started to protest, but Charlotte hushed him.

"I didn't come here to argue," she said. She kissed him softly, slowly, then pulled back and licked her lips. "Mm," she purred. "That's good."

Ed had to have Charlotte. Had to have her before he lost his natural mind. Charlotte knew it. And she sure didn't want him to lose his mind.

He had lied. Told his parents he had to work and would be late to the birthday party. He'd met Charlotte at the bus stop and walked her over. Now she was here and looking so ready, so willing. But he didn't want to rush things, act too eager.

No disrespect to Big Mama, but she'd have plenty of people at her party, piling it on, singing her praises, kissing her ring. Hail to Big Mama, she who knows what's best for everybody. The whole family was one big cult of personality. His own father had bought into it, and he wasn't even a Warford.

Ed figured that he couldn't be the only person who saw the way she treated Crispus. Clearly something about the kid just rubbed her the wrong way. When was someone going to call her on it, the pointed insults and the casual slights? Pristine wasn't going to do it. When Big Mama came back from Florida and brought that one stupid yo-yo with her, the one shaped like two slices of orange, she handed it to Shom like it was made of gold. Left Crisp standing there sad-eyed and empty-handed. Mom told her if she couldn't bring a souvenir for both of them then she shouldn't bring any at all. Big Mama said fine, no more souvenirs. That was the strongest resistance Pristine ever mounted, and it was weak at that. Wasn't Big Mama still bringing Shom presents on the sly? And Reuben, he was too busy breaking Ed's balls to even notice.

Nana and Granddad had a soft spot for Crisp, but they lived out in the country now, too far away to be of much help. Ed tried to do what he could. He used to read comic books with him nearly every weekend, taking time to pore over back issues of *Spider-Man* and *Fantastic Four* while sharing some ice-cold Tahitian Treat. But Ed had a job now, and there was college to think about, and Charlotte too . . .

Big Daddy, now there was a man who loved him some Crispus. He was old-school, so he dug Crisp's paleness. He liked to say that when Crisp was born he looked just like a paper doll. He was not much darker than beige now, but that hair, it was all the way African. In fact, it was just like Big Daddy's. What would Big Daddy think of this Black Is Beautiful stuff?

What would he say to Big Mama's doing so wrong by Crisp? She's always going on about Roderick Bates. Has she ever noticed how smart Crisp is? He's already picked up a lot of French and Spanish from the Genius, makes the both of them stand out. Forget about foreign tongues, people around here don't even speak English anymore—at least the standard kind. It's gotten too white, folks say. It's the Man's language, forced on us when they took away our names and our drums. Hard to figure what's too white and what's not. Some of the kids in the Black Heritage Club had given him grief just for carrying around a Harvard catalog. He was just looking at it, damn.

All his life Ed had been taught that black folks had to be twice as good to be considered half as good. Now some people—well, a lot of people—were saying that we shouldn't measure ourselves by white folks' low standards. They were saying that folks who use dogs and firehoses and billy clubs and broomsticks wrapped in barbed wire and homemade bombs to hurt defenseless little children don't know the first thing about *good*. As comforting and wonderful as this new blackness was, it was also confusing.

Confusing or not, I have some decisions to make before Pop concludes that he can make them for me. Since I'm eating his food and painting his walls and breathing his air. Shoving all this Ivy League crap down my throat, telling me to think about my future. He's one to talk. Who ever heard of a Negro with a college degree opening up a sign shop? True, it was a successful operation, but still. A black man with that all-important piece of paper and what does he do with it? Push a paintbrush.

Ed got up and put on a record. He lowered the tonearm of the humble hi-fi that was passed on to him by his uncle Orville. The needle kissed the groove.

"You are too beautiful, my dear, to be true."

Johnny Hartman. Yeah, that's right, baby, I can be smooth too. I can do more than grunt and sweat and breathe heavy. I got a touch of class. Isn't a touch of class worth a taste of honey?

Ed watched Charlotte as she wandered around his room, picking up objects and putting them down, swaying a little as she let the music get into her. She approached him again and put her hands around his waist. Stood on tiptoes and pressed her center against his.

He'd known he wanted her—no, needed her—the moment he saw her. When she poked her head confidently into the classroom and said she was looking for the Black Heritage Club.

Those plump purple lips. Eyes like Lena Horne's. Perfect teeth and—uh-oh!—a behind to match. A man could lose his natural mind.

Brother Vaughn was quicker that day. He took hold of her arm and escorted her to a seat, grinning like Stepin Fetchit the whole damn time. Ed wasn't worried. He made sure she'd see right away that he was different. Everybody could say a word or two about Martin or Malcolm, maybe even Elijah or Garvey. But who else had read *The Souls of Black Folk* or "The Negro Artist and the Racial Mountain"? Yeah, he gets into Doc Savage and Spider-Man, but that isn't all he reads.

I let the sister know that if she failed to notice me then she was a failure. No getting around it. I spoke up in the meetings, made my uniqueness clear. Talked to her about Nina Simone and Cannonball and Trane while all the knuckleheads were nattering about the Bop, the Deal, or some other dance step. Dance step my ass. Charlotte had to know I was past that jive, that I was down for the serious and nothing else.

Ed and Charlotte took long walks. Held hands and tossed stones into the lake at Fairgrounds Park. Stayed on the phone late at night talking about Vietnam, LBJ, those four little girls in Birmingham. Whether the Devil was Bull Connor or J. Edgar Hoover. Whether or not God had given up on his earthly gig, up and turned his back on us for a while. Charlotte thought he had. Ed wasn't sure.

*R*emember, be smooth, Ed reminded himself. Kissing her, touching her this way, sliding his hands into her slacks, it was difficult to be patient. *Go slow, Ed. Slow.*

I want/I need/I must impress her with my power, stun her with my strength, make a storm break between her thighs. I want to make her scratch my back and scream for Jesus even though she doesn't believe in Him anymore. I want to bump and grind her back to sweet, ferocious belief, fuck her into faith and our Father who art in heaven push push baby oh oh oh you are so *delicious.*

But I need to be gentle.

Even as she peels off her pants. Slides her panties down those legs. Tugs that top over her lovely head. Five feet, four inches of chocolate. Just for me.

I wish I could sleep with her afterward. Hold her like a rock against my dreams.

Sometimes Ed dreams of Curly, sees him falling and falling and falling until thunk! his head hits the curb. Other times he dreams he *is* Curly. He's staggering in the street and wearing Curly's red glasses, but unlike the real Curly he can *see.* Can see Mortimer the cop smiling as he brings his baton down and sends Curly/Ed toppling out of control, hurtling helplessly until Ed sits up in bed and the juju skull lets him know that none of it had been real. None of it had been real except Mortimer's smirk, which said to him: Despite your good grades and your clean fingernails and your faultless Negro work ethic and incomparable home training and your uppity vocabulary, I can bring you to your knees. Whenever and wherever I want. Ed remembers standing petrified on Vandeventer with Brother Charles and Brother Vaughn while Mortimer smirked under the streetlamp less than fifty yards from his house. He remembers thinking, I might die here and I'm so close to home. Pop wants him to go to Harvard after all that?

Charlotte was naked now. The sight of her was itself well worth the lie or two he'd told to make this moment happen. For the touch of her he'd kill, he was sure. Damn, what would he do for a taste?

She motioned for him to take off his clothes. He started peeling them.

Suppose he was foolish enough to go off to Harvard. What if he wandered too far off-campus and right into a gang of rabid Southies? He'd read about the Irish up there, about the famine they ran from and the hatred they ran into once they reached the brave New World. Like every other group of new-comers, they seized on despising blacks as their ticket to membership in that elusive American fantasy. One nation under God, except for the colored.

Hardly anyone said *colored* anymore. Not even the good folks at the NAACP, who were stuck on *Negro*. Nana's generation used a shorthand that he appreciated. They just said "us." No further elaboration necessary. Talking about the west county neighborhood where they both did backbreaking work for a rich white family, Nana and Granddaddy would say, "Not many of us out there. Only ones of us you see are on their way to clean toilets and cut grass." If a heat wave threatened the city's power supply, they'd say, "Guess who's gonna have to deal with dark streets and alleys tonight? Us."

People like to say that we young blacks are obsessed with conspiracy theories; that we see the pale hand of the Man in everything. But where do we get such ideas? Old folks don't merely suspect that electric meters tick faster in the houses of North Gateway, resulting in higher bills; they *know* it. They *know* that the grocers in North Gateway charge twice as much for meat discarded by stores in South Gateway because it had been deemed too old to eat. They know that the basement ward of the city's most prestigious hospital is where they conduct ungodly experiments on "us." The old folks would leave us half-suspecting that white folks dug up the potholes from South Gateway's streets and deposited them all over our side of town before dawn. That is, if they had potholes over there. Even Pop said that you could tell when you crossed over to the South Side because your tires stopped whining. The rock-strewn gully you had been driving on had turned into a street as smooth as a baby's hind part. "Better make sure you can state your business," Pop said, "in case Officer Friendly asks you what you're doing so far from home. And don't let it be night. Ooh, then your goose is cooked fo' sho.'"

Ask old folks for evidence to support their claims and they'd say, "Just keep on living. You'll see."

$\mathcal{E}$d had every intention of continuing to live. For him living had been concentrated and distilled, in essence reduced to an all-encompassing desire that warmed the air, rippled his sheets, and lightly grazed the dark beauty stretched out on his bed. She shivered under his gaze.

He hesitated a minute—but only for a minute—and savored every inch of Charlotte. He wanted to commit to memory everything his eyes took in: the glossy ringlets framing her flawless forehead, the ripe lips sheltering the bright teeth and moist tongue, the round, raisin-tipped breasts, the delicate slope of her belly, the glistening vortex just visible between her sleek thighs. Phenomenal, Ed thought. He lowered himself to the bed, eased his lips next to hers.

"Am I everything you imagined?" Charlotte was coy and confident, a woman aware of her powers.

Ed found it difficult to talk, had no interest in talking. After all this longing, he was down for the serious and nothing else. He forced his lips to part but remained speechless. For once he was all out of adjectives.

Charlotte laughed, satisfied. His dumbstruck stare was

answer enough. She reached for him, leaned back, and spread her legs. Ed became pure hunger. Need hummed in his ears as he held her small head in his hands and gulped her mouth. He moved to her neck, licked and devoured as Charlotte moaned her encouragement. His tongue painted a path between her breasts. He reached under her and wrapped his hands around her rear. It was hot to the touch, slick and graced with a luminous sheen.

Across the room, the album spun on the old hi-fi, forgotten now. Johnny Hartman was still around but preparing to leave, coolly ringing the last changes of "Autumn Serenade." Trane had stretched out on this one, his wistful tenor perfectly matching Hartman's melancholy yearning.

I'll still feel the glow that time cannot fade . . .

Repeat, fade. The tonearm slid across the label and skidded uneasily against the spindle. Bump. Bump. Bump. In uncanny sync with the rhythm being pounded out on the narrow bed, the kiss and crush of loins. Charlotte was the singer now, a soprano grown husky with ardor. Her jazz was a ballad of urgent, liquid lust.

Ed didn't hear Charlotte or the hi-fi, nor did he hear his own ecstatic harmonies. He was immersed in noiseless darkness, lost to all but the wet charms of Charlotte's world. His mind and body rejoicing in the hot wonder of oneness. Briefly, a cogent thought penetrated his celebration of heat. What was that about old folks and living? Never mind all that, I am dying here and happy to go. Leaving Earth now . . .

Straight to heaven, where there is no way I will ever leave. Galloping, surging, flying—melting in the sticky grip of this craving. Loving Charlotte without end, deep in all this goodness.

The Wheat from the Tares

∫pring came early to Sullivan Avenue in 1968, accompanied by a chorus of robins and jubilant bursts of crocuses and tulips.

Pristine knew that her next-door neighbor Rose Whittier had suffered through a rough winter, although the climate had been surprisingly mild. By February it was in the fifties. The unseasonable warmth had been a disappointment to Shom and Crisp, who'd gotten sleds for Christmas. Crisp found some solace in the new Orlando Cepeda first baseman's mitt he'd begged for all winter, despite the fact that, as Shom constantly reminded him, he was far too short to be anybody's first baseman. The boys were free to play catch in the backyard as long as they stayed out of the vegetable garden and the flower beds. On spring afternoons, Pristine gardened while the boys practiced, and on her second-floor back porch, Rose took in the sun. She turned her face this way and that, reveling in the warm golden rays.

Pristine imagined the weather was drastically different next door in Rose's flat, most likely blustery and cold. Sometimes on midnight journeys to relieve a bladder weakened by childbirth, she couldn't help hearing Paul shouting and swearing and God knows what else, followed by Rose sobbing. Once Pristine woke Reuben and suggested that they call the police, but he in turn suggested that she mind her own business.

Wasn't that what she was always telling him when he wanted to go out and investigate every dropped bottle, muffled shout, or mysterious bang that he heard?

Come spring, when day broke and the increasingly disheveled Paul staggered off—late—to his job at the plant, Rose liked to sunbathe on her back porch and feed her pet rabbit, a gift from Paul in happier days. Hugging the animal close, she lifted her eyes heavenward, and slowly, magically, the sound worked its way from the depths of her soul. Rose's repertoire varied, but she usually began with something a resident of North Gateway was likely to hear on any given Sunday. Something like

> *I tol' Jesus it would be all right*
> *If He changed mah name.*
> *Jesus tol' me I would have to live humble*
> *If He changed mah name.*

Rose's voice was an extraordinary thing, an effortless blend of longing, power, and love. It reminded Pristine of her grandmother, whose plaintive hymns had resonated through the house on late summer evenings when Pristine was a teenager, sitting close to Reuben on her family's front porch.

The two of them had gone off to Jefferson University together, continuing their high school romance. She'd had two years of biology under her belt when she dropped out and got married. It was the end of a promising academic career, but she had no regrets: God had blessed her. Reuben was as gifted as any man and prone, like any man, to fits of temper. But he'd never laid a hand on her. The strong, silent type until you got to know him, he eventually revealed himself as the rascal he was. He was a jock in the early days and a bit of a show-off.

Once at the Pine Street Y, he launched a somersault off the high dive to impress her. Somehow he hit his foot against the side of the board and lost his form way above the water. It led to a frightening descent that he managed to limp away from, leaving a huge knot on the side of his foot that still gives him pain. In their more playful moods, he'd rub the sore spot and tell her that he knew firsthand that love was a hurting thing. "Talking about your little toe?" she'd tease. "Compared to having a baby it must ache something awful."

Reuben worked hard, and she always knew where he was. When he wasn't at the Black Swan, he was in that firetrap of a studio down in the basement. No matter how busy he got on the job, she could always count on him to come through the door with her cigarettes and pumpkin seeds, right on time. Every Sunday, to his kids' delight, he brought them ice cream from Horack's Dairy, a tradition they began when it was just the two of them and Ed in that little flat on Emerson Avenue.

Pristine dedicated herself to creating the kind of family life she and Reuben had often dreamed of during those front-porch sessions. Working part-time at a department store and selling Avon allowed her to be at home, waiting with hugs and kisses, when her children arrived from school.

She fancied herself a collector of memories: Late at night, with her pumpkin seeds and Belair Lights at her side, she assembled scrapbooks. She had volumes of them by the beginning of 1968. Every photo—they had hundreds—every report card, every childhood scribble, every milk tooth and lock of hair was carefully glued into place.

Pristine used to bring out a little radio and set it down beside her. *Tent Meeting with Rev. Josiah Banks* kept her company as she hung the laundry or weeded. Most spring days the radio sat silent in deference to the singer next door as Pristine busied herself. In contrast, Rose never seemed to have enough to do. The two women exchanged warm "Good mornings" when Rose came out to feed her rabbit, although Rose's smile was always brief. Pristine would be clipping sheets to the line or tending her tulips and crocuses when the sound would begin. It started out angelic and sweet, then quickly grew loud, mystically amplified as if some circuitry was hidden in Rose's throat.

Occasionally, Pristine would put down her trowel and shield her eyes to steal a glimpse at Rose's plump, ecstatic face. When the feeling overtook Rose, she'd shuck her customary shyness, stand and grab the porch railings. Her voice would pour out over the garage roofs, garbage cans, and backyards of Sullivan Avenue. Pristine would later swear that the entire neighborhood grew quiet to give Rose center stage. Gone was the sound of trucks and buses belching exhaust along nearby Vandeventer Avenue. Into thin air went the leonine roars of the Dobermans standing guard behind Hudson's Package Liquor. Everything that had made the world teeming with noise just moments before vanished.

She sang "His Eye Is on the Sparrow" and the birds respectfully hushed their twittering. She sang "Didn't It Rain" and you could just see the Flood, torrents of water washing over the bricks and rising up to the ash pits lining the alley, sweeping sinner and saint alike in its holy current. She sang "God's Gonna Separate the Wheat from the Tares" and the flowers stretched their stems and leaned into the sound.

She sang only when her husband wasn't home. The silence that followed his arrival was not a kind that encouraged peaceful contemplation; it was troubling and electric, like calm before a storm. Paul used to at least pretend to be a gospel singer, but months had passed since he last lifted his voice in song. He left with lunch kit and hard hat in hand, but Claude Mays, the kind, fastidious man who lived across the street, claimed to have seen him at the racetrack during working hours. Once, Paul had nearly knocked Crispus down on the way home from school. He was sprinting furiously, eyes bugged out and spittle flying from his open mouth. To Crispus, the running man looked as if he'd seen a creature from another dimension, and he found no comfort in discovering that grown-ups had ghost issues too. Other days, Mrs. Cleveland spotted Paul shooting craps behind Chink's. One of the most notable of the neighborhood's many eccentrics, Mrs. Cleveland missed nothing. A Coca-Cola addict, she went through two dozen bottles a day and swept her front walk constantly, her hair tied up in a scarf, her hands hidden in work gloves. Her property was so well-kept that strangers occasionally drove by and took pictures of her house. "Nothing but a sinner," Mrs. Cleveland said of Paul.

Pristine was snapping pole beans one Saturday morning when she heard Paul shouting. "I said stop making all that god-damned noise!" The Whittiers' screen door slapped open and Rose stepped out on the porch. Her arms were folded and she was humming softly.

Pristine called to her ballplaying boys. "Shom! Crispus! Go inside."

"But, Mom," Crisp protested. "We're working on our pick-off moves."

"Inside now," she commanded. "Move your hind parts. Go!"

Muttering objections, the boys slunk past their mother and went inside.

Next door, Paul followed his wife onto the porch. "When I tell you to shut up, I mean it," he said, loud enough for the whole world to hear. Rose never turned around to face him.

She leaned over the railing, closed her eyes, and sang. There was something different in her tone, defiance maybe.

> *My Lord, what a morning!*
> *My Lord, what a morning!*
> *Oh, my Lord, what a morning*
> *when the stars begin to fall.*

"I'm gon' tell you just one more time!"

> *Oh, you will hear the trumpet sound*
> *to wake the nations underground,*
> *Looking to my Lord's right hand*
> *when the stars begin—*

"No, Paul! Don't!"

Pristine watched Paul raise Rose's beloved rabbit above his head. Leaning over the railing, he hurled the animal downward with all his considerable strength.

"He murdered the little critter in cold blood. I saw it all," Pristine later told Reuben. "I stood up in spite of myself, spilling pole beans all over the porch. The rabbit made that same snapping sound I used to hear when my grandma wrung a chicken's neck.

" 'I told you to shut your mouth,' he said. You should have heard the noise Rose made, Reub. The most awful sound you ever heard. It was like when she sings but backward, like she was sucking all the light and joy back into herself, where it would never be seen or felt again. Her breath seemed to pull dark clouds from all over Gateway. Maybe the sun moved a bit too. That kind of noise doesn't belong anywhere near good people and I never want to hear it again, Reub. Never."

That night Pristine called Polly's mom and asked her to bake a lemon pie. Mrs. Garnett dropped it off the following morning.

An hour later, Pristine pressed Rose's doorbell. She waited, then pressed again. Finally, she leaned on the button. After a long pause, Rose shouted from the top of the stairs.

"Who is it?"

"It's Pristine Jones, from next door."

"Is everything all right?"

"I was planning to ask you the same thing."

"Why would you ask that?"

"I was in my yard yesterday when—I saw—Thought we could talk. You know, instead of shouting through this thick door."

"My husband doesn't like for me to have company."

"I know that, but he isn't home. I brought some lemon pie."

Pristine heard Rose making her way down the stairs. How many locks does a door need? she wondered as Rose turned dead bolt after dead bolt and released the chain.

She was still pretty, despite everything. She even tried to smile, although it clearly hurt for her to do so. Rose had on a pale blue housecoat and curlers in her hair.

"Good morning," Pristine said.

"Morning. Come in. Forgive me, I wasn't expecting visitors. And my house—"

"Child, please. You should see mine. Reuben says if I spent as much time in the house as I do in the yard, everything would be spick-and-span."

"He shouldn't say that," Rose said as they mounted the stairs. "You've got those fine boys to look after."

When they reached the top of the stairs, Pristine discovered that her hostess was just being modest. You could have eaten off her floors. Everything gleamed like a Glo-Coat commercial, from the waxed linoleum kitchen floor to the impossibly bad portrait of Rose and Paul above the mantel in the living room.

"Paul likes things just so," Rose explained. "Inside, I mean. Outside, well, he doesn't like me in the yard. I would be perfectly happy hanging clothes out there like I see you doing, but he bought me a big dryer and said I darn well better use it." Rose smiled again. "But he didn't say darn."

"I haven't gotten used to those things myself," Pristine said. "I prefer God's light."

Rose nodded. "God's light. Who doesn't like that?"

"You, I'm guessing. You got all your blinds closed on such a beautiful day."

"Every day that the Lord sends is beautiful. I don't need to look out the window to know that. Besides, I prefer to take my sun on the back porch. I like to sit out there and marvel on God's creation. To think that He made every blade of grass, every rock and pebble. I like to sit out there with Twitchy. That's my rabbit."

Pristine looked in Rose's eyes and saw her remembering. Saw her recalling Paul's yelling, the rabbit tumbling through space.

"I'm sorry," Rose said quickly. "I'm forgetting my manners. Please have a seat. Can I get you some coffee? I can't wait to taste this pie."

"I've had my coffee for today. But some milk would be nice."

Rose poured milk into a glass, sliced the pie, and served it. She was not a small woman, but she moved like one. All her gestures were neat and dainty.

"Umm, this is good, Pristine. I mean Mrs. Jones."

"You were right the first time. Call me Pristine. A friend of mine made it. I've tried to do her recipe, but I keep missing something somehow."

Rose set her fork on her saucer. "I want to apologize for all the noise my husband makes. Sometimes he feels a lot of anger."

"All men feel anger, honey. The smart ones find someplace to put it." Pristine thought of the abstract charcoal sketches Reuben made after Ed saw Curly die. They were full of slashes and short, sharp lines, as if Reuben had been stabbing the paper.

"He didn't used to be so mad. I met him and his brothers at a gospel showdown. They got to do two numbers right before the Staple Singers came on. They looked so handsome in their double-breasted suits, and their harmonies were *tight*. Paul was full of himself but full of dreams too. He and his brothers were going to be as big as the Four Tops, but they would stick to the holy road. None of that Sam Cooke trespassing for them. Cooke crossed over, and look what it got him. God don't like ugly, Paul said. He was a different Paul then, before he got . . . distracted. Now he's always out in the streets. I tell myself that's all right as long as he comes home."

"I suppose there's something to that," Pristine began. "But it's not just about him being home. It's about what he does while he's here."

Rose thought about Paul stumbling in smelling of liquor. Sometimes he sprawled across the bed and began to snore without even taking off his boots. At least then he wasn't cursing and yelling or—worse yet—balling up his fists. The only problem was she felt alone all the time, whether he was home or not.

"You and your husband go out much?"

Pristine licked meringue from her lips. "We've never been the going-out type. There's not money for that anyway, so we try to keep it simple. The kids think going downtown for pancakes at Woolworth's is a big deal. Sometimes, when the little ones have gone to sleep, Reuben surprises me with shrimp from High Wheels or a middle cut from Dempsey Wynne's. Our routines are familiar, and that might seem boring to some. But it's helpful too."

"How is that?"

"After all this time we can communicate without speaking. We know each other's mind."

This time Rose's smile struggled to settle on her face. It quickly vanished as she appeared to choke down something bitter. Pristine noticed but said nothing.

"Mind, huh? Half the time I'm not sure I got one."

"Hmmph. Anybody who sings like you has got to have a mind."

"I don't have to think to do that. It comes from my soul."

"Soul, mind. I'm not sure there's a difference. But I'm sure you have one. Now, peace of mind? You should ask yourself about that."

Pristine feared overstepping her bounds. At the same time, she wanted to be sure that she'd made her point. She didn't know if she'd get another chance to cross Rose's threshold.

"Rose, you've been on our block two years now. Some folks know your voice, but hardly anyone knows your face or your name. Don't you think it's time you met your neighbors? Reuben and I like to sit outside some evenings with the Collinses. They're good people, and you may have noticed that they seldom leave their porch. Claude Mays is that dapper little man who lives across the street. He's a tailor. Never been married, and there's a reason for that. His landlord is Mrs. Cleveland. She can't keep still, but she's harmless. You've seen Mrs. Scott three doors down? Everybody calls her Aunt Georgia. She sleeps with a gun under her pillow and she doesn't like to be surprised. You must have seen Mrs. O'Gwynn across the alley. You can see her yard real good from your porch."

"I've seen her," Rose agreed. "She's always arguing with her dog."

"Yes, he's named Shame. He's loud, but that's about it. But the old lady herself is a storyteller. A regular raconteur, my Reuben would say. I'm telling you, she should have been in show business. I remember a story she told me when I first moved on the block. She told me she knew someone back in Mississippi whose husband was one crazy cuss."

Rose raised an eyebrow above the coffee cup she held to her lips.

"Used to beat the woman something awful," Pristine continued. "Seems like he was bound and determined to break her spirit, take all her joy away."

Rose lifted her fork to her mouth but thought better of it. She set it back down.

"One day he beat her and he went to sleep. She went to the kitchen and turned on the stove. The way Mrs. O'Gwynn tells it, the man wakes up after a while and smells bacon frying. He smiles to himself and stretches out in the bed. What a good woman, he thinks. I beat her and now all she wants to do is feed me."

Rose's tongue found the loosened molar in her upper jaw, pressed it into place. She wasn't aware that she did that dozens of times each day.

"It turns out that the woman had no intention of filling her husband's belly. She filled his ears instead. Waited until he was good and asleep and tied him to the bed. Poured hot bacon grease in his ears. He cursed and screamed, but it did him no good."

"Did he die?"

"Don't know. But I suspect he learned his lesson."

Rose stood up. Her hands were trembling, so she pressed them to the table to steady them. "That's a terrible story," she said, her voice breaking.

Pristine knew her time was up. "It's just a story," she said. "I don't even know why I recalled it just now. I didn't come over here to tell it."

"What did you come over here for, to tell me to leave my husband? I took a vow."

"I see. And he didn't?"

Silence hung between the two women like a veil. Finally, Pristine spoke.

"I thought you could use a friend, Rose. Maybe I'm not that friend, but you'll never make one if you don't leave the house. There's a community rally coming up at Good Samaritan. Maybe you'd like to come. The Justice Singers are supposed to show. Please, just think about it."

"All right," Rose said quickly. "I will."

Later, when Pristine told Reuben about her visit next door, she didn't mention the bacon.

"A community rally? You haven't even been to one yourself."

"Doesn't mean I can't start. I'm a member of the community, so I'm invited. Anyway, I don't know if she'll think about it at all. I do know that she would have said just about anything to get me out of her house."

As time passed, an uneasy peace rode the reliable spring currents breezing through the women's backyards. Rose sang, Pristine gardened and minded her rambunctious boys, and occasionally the women's eyes met above the fence. The looks they exchanged grew warmer in time, and Pristine imagined the two of them had reached some kind of understanding. Rose felt something else entirely on her part, something more like a mildly obsessive jealousy that she wasn't proud of. She took to keeping up with the Joneses, noting their noisy comings and goings, the boisterous pattern of their days. She knew on Friday evenings they ventured to Kroger and came back loaded down with groceries and Top Value trading stamps. Sundays she pictured them enjoying the ice cream Reuben brought from Horack's Dairy.

But her favorites were the ordinary days, the ones devoted to no particular occasion or cause. She found something to do on her porch as dusk descended, or hovered unseen just inside her screen door and watched the boys stretch for errant tossed balls in the gathering shadows; she spied Pristine expertly retrieving her crisp, sun-bleached sheets, plucking them from the line, folding and settling them in her wicker laundry basket in what appeared to be a single compact, graceful motion, then pausing at the sound of a car entering from the near end of the alley, a clothespin hanging from lips already blooming into a lovely, expectant smile. Pristine even knew the sound of her husband's engine, the stubborn wheeze of his carburetor as he backed the Rambler wagon into the battered garage.

Rose looked on steadily as Reuben, paint-spattered and sweaty, gathered the tools of his trade, stacked them on his jerry-rigged yet reliable shelves, and stepped into the yard with all the enthusiasm of a saint at the gates of heaven. If it wasn't too dark, a miraculous streak of sun sometimes found his gold tooth and gave his grin a mischievous glint. Soon enough his wiry arms were stretched around two laughing boys and a loving wife. Rose saw it all, craned her neck to follow them as they ambled through the back door and disappeared into the golden glow of the Jones kitchen. She breathed deeply, as if her neighbors' affection gave off an aroma to savor, like the ribs Reuben was fond of grilling over hickory on summer nights.

Rose acquired the habit of eating her solitary dinners near her kitchen window. The Joneses kept their shades low, but their shadows could be seen from time to time. Hungrily watching their silhouettes, Rose pictured them eating at the table, inhaling satisfying mouthfuls of Pristine's lovingly prepared dishes between warmhearted exchanges and laughter-filled recollections of busy, fulfilling days. Reuben was probably describing some kooky character he'd bumped into while dropping Ed off at SuperMart, or a fender bender he'd witnessed while touching up the sign in front of Yeatman Clinic. From time to time, she knew, the sign painter reached out and rubbed the nappy heads of his boys. Or extended his strong fingers and touched his wife's hand for no reason at all.

As evenings lengthened into the depth of night, shadows no longer danced behind the shades next door. Long after the younger boys had been bathed and put to bed and Reuben and Pristine had shared a can of Stag and watched Max Roby deliver the final newscast of the night, Rose would move across her desolate flat to the front window. Sometimes she'd sit there and stare out at the dark, quiet houses of Sullivan Avenue. The streetlights might occasionally shine on a lonesome traveler, maybe Austin Burk, the undertaker's scary son, or Talk Much, the long-limbed, laconic man who sometimes worked with Reuben. He was known to stop and place his palm against the edge of a building as if taking its pulse. Talk Much? Walk Much was more like it, Rose thought. A few doors west, an occasional car would roll down Vandeventer Avenue, a recalcitrant muffler ruffling the stillness. What did Paul's car sound like? That would be a good thing to know.

It also would be nice to know what Pristine had that she didn't. Her well-meaning neighbor wasn't bad-looking, especially when she smiled. But Pristine was thin, while she, Rose, was what admiring men liked to call a healthy girl. Childbearing hips, she'd heard the girl watchers whisper on those brief, rare occasions when daylight found her roaming free. Hips to keep a man warm at night. How Paul used to love to stroke those hips, curves that had known the touch of no other man. They used to talk about making a baby—a girl, Rose often predicted. They'd name her Marie, Rose's favorite name in the whole world. Nowadays Paul seldom looked at her, except maybe to determine exactly where to place his fist. Who would bother to look at her now? Who would see beneath the welts and bruises?

That man outside Curly's funeral had looked at her. Gabriel had looked *in* her, or so it had seemed for a strange, disconcerting moment. He'd made her feel naked as Eve and just as shameful. And what did she have to be ashamed about? All she'd done was sing a joyful noise unto the Lord.

On such nights, curled up in her chair near the window, Rose would wrap her arms around herself and nod. Her chin bumped against her chest as weariness overtook her. The hiss of the radiators gave way to imagined murmurings, soft lips and warm hands, babies with flake-gold eyes. And finally, the sweetness of sleep.

Planning the Perfect Evening

*e*verything was going bad. Nothing made sense anymore. No one showed up when they said they would. No one believed him when he said he was good for whatever he owed. Everywhere he looked he saw Guts Tolliver's fat reflection. He was convinced the leg breaker had spies watching him from high in the trees, monitoring his movements from chimney tops and alleyways. Clinging to the shadows no longer helped.

When he finally crept from the darkness and made it up the stairs of his immaculate home, he often found Rose sitting in the kitchen, staring out the window as if she was watching TV. Nothing to see but the neighbors' yellowing, tattered shade.

She hardly moved when he came in, her relaxed, splendidly indifferent posture practically begging him to slap some sense into her, as if that was possible. He rolled up his sleeves and stepped toward her without so much as a "Honey, I'm home." Time was, a woman hopped up and made herself busy when her man came through the door. Time was, insolence didn't go steaming out of a woman like sewer gas. Where was she getting this new, foul attitude? True, he kept her nosy ass out of his business, but that gave her no excuse for not being able to tell that he was in distress. That he had concerns beyond her understanding.

Rose suddenly snapped alert, as if waking from an absorbing dream. She looked at him like she'd never seen him before, had never rocked him to ecstasy between her thighs. She recovered, curving her lips from round surprise to smiling recognition, but she was too slow. He was drunk but not too tore up to miss her momentary confusion.

"You look tired, Paul," she said. "You need some rest. Come on, let me run you a bath. Get some food in you and lie down."

"I never loved you anyway. Everybody was always talking about your voice. Your goddamned voice."

Rose winced. "Stop it, Paul."

"I said, I'll fix that. I'll shut that bitch up even if I have to marry her."

"Paul, that's not true."

"You didn't think I really wanted you, did you? What you got I can get anywhere. I'm Paul Whittier, don't you know."

He needed to get to her before she started that awful warbling. She'd taken to singing even while he slapped her plump jaws, split her lips—again—beneath his knuckles. Did she think a few lilting notes would stay his hand? She had another think coming.

Stinking up Rose's bed, his long, boot-clad feet smearing mud across her intensely vacuumed throw rug, his hands still throbbing from giving the ball and chain exactly what she needed, Paul settled into his evening snore. He burrowed his stubbly jaw into his pillow, trying mightily to resist the lure of a tantalizing scent emanating from the kitchen. Through the fog of his alcohol-soaked breath and the belligerent bite of his festering B.O., he struggled to identify the source of the aroma. Just as he descended into the best sleep he'd known in weeks, the answer landed lightly, perfectly on the tip of his tongue: bacon.

*C*lub, cutlass, pliers, band saw, broomstick, garrote, piano wire, pistol, dagger, box cutter, baseball bat, his own 14 EEE work brogans, a lace from said brogans, chopsticks, ice pick, knitting needles, straight razor, brass knuckles, *his* knuckles, a crutch, the crook of his arm—it was easier to conceive of a weapon that Guts Tolliver had not used to dispatch some unfortunate soul to the hereafter than to establish with certainty a comprehensive catalog of his instruments of death.

Guts's upper lip was clean-shaven, but his bounteous jaws sported a thick fringe of beard that brought to mind portraits of those black senators and congressmen who dared to darken the legislative branch for a brief, tantalizing span following the Civil War. It also brought to mind a certain six-hundred-pound wrestler who wore sofa-size overalls and carried a giant horseshoe into the ring. Guts's resemblance to Hayseed the Magnificent was a source of not pride but discomfort, and the fact of his anguish was made abundantly clear through a sensational and bone-chilling demonstration of the versatility of the shoelace. Guts was picking up a pair of freshly polished wingtips for his employer at the shine parlor next to Curly's confectionery when a low-level denizen of Gateway's underworld—known for all eternity as "that damn fool"—greeted the corpulent assassin with a "What's happenin', Hayseed?" Folks known to hang out thereabouts swear up and down that the parlor's proprietors are still scraping up what's left of that late, unlamented, loose-tongued simpleton. If anyone had found the temerity to ask Guts himself about the incident, he simply would have shrugged and admitted that he didn't sweat the details.

Not that Guts didn't have a tender side. That very aspect of his complex, unpredictable personality took hold of him as he wheeled his Plymouth toward the western end of Sullivan Avenue. He was planning the perfect evening, which for him always included the same two indispensable ingredients, Pearl Jordan and banana pudding. Pearl was as petite as Guts was grand ("gross," some might think but never say out loud) and admirably undaunted by the eventful journey to his heart that the vast, uncharted reaches of his midsection promised. Guts had long ago given up the pleasures of being on top—led to that epiphany by a pair of brave but shallow lasses who found themselves nearly loved to death beneath his immeasurable folds—and learned to accept satisfaction where he found it. Not even Guts dreamed that joy would arrive in a lifelong companion who practiced twirling atop her mountainous man until she could ride him to mutually transporting extremes, pausing at appropriate intervals to lean forward and lovingly spoon more banana pudding into his happy, waiting mouth.

His previous surveys of Paul's block, conducted under a hard hat and with the assistance of an ostentatious clipboard, had enabled him to ascertain that the man's front door was barricaded by an inordinate number of locks. He soon deduced that the padlocks, chains, and dead bolts were intended not to hold the world at bay but to keep his wife in. She was lovely, Guts had seen, although a bit round for his tastes. But hey, to each his own, right?

The basement door in back of the Whittier residence was little more than reinforced plywood and could be torn from its hinges if locks turned out to be a problem. He could kick it in with an expertly placed 14 EEE or subdue it with a muted grunt and a wedge of shoulder, but he chose instead to just lean on it, rub the coarse grain, and mumble sweet nothings until it popped open as easily as a Washington Avenue whore.

And he was in. He spied a pull chain above the husky shadow of the clothes dryer and gave it a tug. Used the amber glare to make his way to the stairs.

Some claimed Guts Tolliver was light on his feet, a nimble-toed wonder of aerodynamic bulk. Whoever heard such talk reserved judgment, preferring to see such a marvel before stamping it with the official seal of belief. Rose failed to witness Guts's miraculous manipulation of space because her back was turned when he materialized in her kitchen. Trancelike she flipped the bacon with a large, two-tined fork, oblivious to the random pops of hot grease. Then she was all too aware of the giant standing just a pounce away, a great gloved finger pressed to his generous, oddly sensual lips. She briefly considered defending herself with the fork before quickly realizing it would snap feebly before penetrating even the second layer of the stranger's abundant flesh.

The ogre in her kitchen had the nerve to tip his hat.

"Lord Jesus," she said. "Please don't hurt me."

"No danger of that, ma'am. Besides, looks like somebody's already done that." Embarrassed, Rose touched a hand to her blackened eye.

Guts wrapped Rose's neck in the crook of his arm as casually as a letterman escorting his sweetheart to the homecoming dance. He was still holding her that way when he steered her into the bedroom and roused Paul with his foot.

"Let's go, fella," Guts said. "I'm tired of playing hide-and-seek. Aren't you?"

Paul blinked in terror. He wanted to be dreaming. Guts could almost hear him making those bargains he'd heard countless times in similar situations. Please God, he was thinking, begging. Please let me be dreaming.

But no.

"I'm not going to kill you, Paul. However, I do have orders. My employer wants you and me . . . to have a little discussion."

Paul said nothing. He looked at Rose, then at Guts. He considered offering his wife's body for his freedom or, failing that, her life for his. Rose read his face and saw him weighing the options. Paul saw that she understood, and in that moment they both were lost.

Paul yanked the alarm clock from the nightstand and hurled it at the intruder's head. Guts ducked gracefully (he was used to that sort of thing), at the same time gently nudging Rose's head and shoulders beneath the trajectory of the clock as it hit the wall and shattered.

"Time really does fly, doesn't it, Paul?"

Guts was especially proud of that pun, but he restrained himself out of respect for the wife. He released her, picked Paul up by the nape of his neck, and headed toward the back stairs.

"Call the police!" Paul shouted.

"Don't do that, ma'am," Guts advised. "Right now only Paul's in trouble. My employer has no quarrel with you."

Rose nodded.

"And, ma'am?"

"Y-yes?"

"I do believe that bacon's burning."

Returning to her trance, Rose turned off the stove. She faced the kitchen window, tuning out the sound of her husband being bumped and stumbled down the stairs. Staring at her neighbors' yellowing and tattered shade, she lowered herself into her chair.

Standing between Guts and Guts's car tucked neatly behind the garage next door, Paul understood that he had nowhere to run. Helplessly, he began to whimper.

Guts sighed. He reached into the waistband of his pants and, to Paul's puzzled horror, retrieved a peppermint candy. He leisurely unwrapped it and tossed it into his mouth. "Now, Paul," he said. "I'm going to tell you a couple things about me. I love a woman named Pearl. I have had men in your position do exactly what you thought about doing a few minutes ago. In their desperation, they offer me their wives, their mothers. Some of them even offer their daughters, Paul. I always turn them down, and you know why? Not out of some exalted sense of morality. I turn them down because I have a woman and I'm satisfied with her. I love her. The other thing to know about me? I love banana pudding. Not the kind that comes in a box, understand. My Pearl makes it in a big stainless-steel bowl. Well, not a bowl exactly. It's actually a pot but the handle's fallen off. Anyway, Pearl puts vanilla wafers all around and tops it off with homemade meringue. You see? Pearl, pudding. Pudding, pearl. That's all I need in this world. Tonight I plan to see my woman and she plans to give me . . . my just deserts."

Guts was awfully proud of that pun, but he restrained himself because no small degree of subtlety is required when jamming a dirty rag in your captive's mouth, binding his wrists and ankles with electrical cord, and stuffing all six feet, one inch of him into the trunk of your Plymouth.

The car had barely rolled the length of the alley and busted a hard left onto Prairie Avenue when Ed Jones dragged the family trash cans to the alley for morning pickup. He turned and looked up and down the alley because he was sure he'd heard an engine idling, seen the twinkle of a taillight, and maybe even caught a mouthful of garbled sentences. But now there was nothing. Just an empty stretch of alley and the intermittent fussing of Shame, Mrs. O'Gwynn's irritable dog.

Guts was headed to the river. Above its sullen, brown

depths stretched the Poplar Street Bridge, a fabled expanse of steel dividing one racially polarized, Dixie-flavored midwestern state from another. His employer's instructions called for depositing the passenger in his trunk on the far side of the state line and prohibiting him from troubling the Gateway side ever again. He'd pay with his kneecaps and not his life because the boss had a soft spot for him, got a kick out of watching him the way a bunch of sadistic third-graders watch a hamster toiling away on his wheel. The boss derived welcome distraction from seeing Paul run and run and run, knowing all the while there was no way out.

At the intersection of Delmar and Finney, Guts had to stomp the brakes when a young black man sprang from nowhere and darted across the street. He'd barely registered that event when a police cruiser came screaming through, siren blasting and beacons ablaze.

"Chasing a black man in black clothes on a black night," Guts said aloud. "Good luck with that."

At the docks, Guts backed his Plymouth to the edge of the water. He retrieved his fretful bundle and dumped it on the stones. "Paul," he said. "Did you know that W. C. Handy slept on these very stones when he first came to Gateway?" It was a speech he'd given before. Guts reached under the driver's seat and found his trusty length of pipe, to which he'd attached a finger-friendly grip normally used on a bicycle's handlebar.

"He was poor and hungry and had nowhere to sleep. You're keeping good company, friend. But this is where you and I part ways. I got to get a move on because I'm hungry and I also have to take a tinkle."

That a man so massively masculine and robustly rotund would favor a delicate word like *tinkle* struck even Guts as a tad incongruous. He'd inherited it from his beloved mother, who shared both Guts's dimensions and his fondness for jokes. He'd experimented with coarser words—blue-collar, labor-union words like *piss* and *whiz*. But he always found himself returning to the euphemisms of childhood. So *tinkle* it was.

Paul's eyes gleamed hugely in the moonlight.

"You can't cross over to the Gateway side ever again. Not for any reason at all, got it?"

Paul nodded violently. Guts took one practice swing, then another. "If you are foolish enough to cross over, Paul, it won't be on foot. I'm going to make sure of that."

Guts noticed wetness spreading across the front of Paul's pants. He sighed.

"Looks like I'm not the only one who had to go. Watch the boots, huh, Paul?"

Lives of the Artists

*W*hile Guts handled his business and dreamed of banana pudding, the men of the Black Swan hung out late. Above their heads swirled the fumes and scents that defined their comfort: paint, turpentine, coffee, tobacco, Skin Bracer, smoke.

Bob Cobb, a round, amiable gentleman, wore a knee-length lab smock that was probably white once. It was covered with lackluster splotches of gunmetal gray, lurid splashes of neon orange, silver, and indigo. An aura of goodwill glowing from his shiny, nearly bald scalp, he puffed contentedly on a pipe and watched Reuben match wits with George West over a checkerboard that had clearly seen better days. Both combatants held foam cups filled with steaming black coffee.

Tall and taciturn, Talk Much presided over an ancient hi-fi teetering in a corner, from which issued the unmistakable sound of Chuck Berry expressing his impatience with Maybellene. Lucius Monday, hunched over a large drafting table, actually an old door balanced on a couple of sawhorses, was the only man working. Every now and then he'd look up and comment on the checkers game with a jocularity that belied his intimidating appearance.

He was dark and rough-skinned. A long, unruly beard, a blend of coal dust and cotton, connected the deep scars on either side of his wide nose to a pair of spectacularly bloodshot eyes. In the center of his beard sat a fat and equally crimson slice of bottom lip. He held in one hand a sign painter's tool called a maulstick, a length of wood that looked like a sawed-off bamboo fishing pole. A round, uneven ball made of rags and tape was stuck to the other end of the stick, held there by a looped and knotted tangle of twine. His other hand, grasping a brush with the light, sure touch of a surgeon wielding a scalpel, applied the finishing touches to a sign declaring "20% Off!"

Between moves, Reuben and West discussed their attempts to collect a debt from a delinquent client. Forced to toil without the services of a proven accounts manager of the Guts Tolliver variety, the men of the Black Swan sometimes found themselves at the mercy of the North Side's most elusive characters.

"Boudreau's most likely not going to pay," Monday predicted.

"I doubted that punch-drunk chump from the get-go," West said. "We're never going to see that money."

They were talking about Jerome "the Creole Crusher" Boudreau, who almost fought a championship bout once. He had a TV repair shop on Prairie Avenue.

"Monday and I went over there two days ago," Reuben said. "I had called first to tell him we were on our way over, which was probably a mistake. We get there and nothing's going on inside. No lights on. We ring the bell, bang on the glass, nobody answers."

"Suddenly I make out something moving," Monday interjects, "a shadow moving in the semidarkness. Turns out it's Boudreau crawling around on his hands and knees, hoping we don't see him."

"I feel sorry for him," said Bob Cobb. "In his prime, he was a real contender. One of the best fighters I've ever seen."

"I've seen better," Reuben said. "The best I ever saw used to skirmish in the back of my uncle's Laundromat. They were rats, understand. Big, rowdy-looking rodents. They'd actually stand on their hind legs and trade punches."

Over at the hi-fi, Talk Much chuckled and started the record over.

Bob Cobb had introduced his tight-lipped friend to the others some years ago, after Reuben had admired Talk Much's spectacular handling of the giant feline gracing the front of Katz Drugs. "Whoever did that sign is operating on a whole other level," he had surmised.

"That there is the handiwork of Talk Much, formerly known as Ronald Ewing," Cobb explained. "But it's been a long time since he answered to that. A real artistic genius, that one. Planets and prophecies bloomed from the end of his brush. Had a full scholarship to Grambling. A life of promise and potential just waiting for him to jump up and seize the day."

"Get to the point if you got one," West had urged. He could talk without parting his teeth.

Reuben glared at West, but Cobb blithely ignored him. "His woman left him. Name was Karintha. Pretty as a picture. Curls fat and greasy as strips of bacon. She was with him through college and two years of the service. Six years, all told, until he found her in the arms of another man."

"That's terrible," Reuben said. West just rolled his eyes.

"Lucius and I have seen her," Cobb said. "Talk still carries her picture in his wallet."

"I wouldn't say she was so pretty," Monday said. "That mustache would have distracted me."

"She did not have a mustache," said Cobb. "She had a dusky upper lip, that's all."

"So he's been screwed up ever since?" Reuben asked, staring up at the sign and half-expecting the huge, realistic whiskers to start trembling in the breeze.

"I prefer to say he occasionally has problems maintaining sobriety," Cobb replied.

Monday nodded sympathetically. He knew something about that too.

Talk Much joined the crew soon after. Now he swayed lightly above the rickety stereo while Chuck Berry's beloved broke his heart again.

Cobb snorted. "Man, get outta here with that John Brown jive."

John Brown jive was Swan-speak for b.s.

West rolled his eyes. "Stop lying, Reub, and concentrate on this game before I dethrone your prevaricating ass."

"I'm telling the truth as sure as I'm sitting here with four ugly fellas," Reuben rejoined.

West was a skinny, sharp-nosed man dressed in dungarees and pointy-toed, paint-stained cowboy boots. His big, bushy mustache vibrated when he spoke. Setting down his coffee cup, West picked up his pipe, placed it between his clenched teeth, and lighted it. After a few preliminary puffs, he exhaled a plume of smoke. "Myself," he began, "I've had an encounter with rodents too. Some of them set up living quarters in a box in my basement, without seeking my permission or negotiating a reasonable rental fee."

"What did you do?" Lucius asked.

West could hardly wait to reply. "I slid that box out the back door, all the way to the alley. Tossed some gasoline on that sucker and set it on fire. I could hear them rats frying, understand. Hopping and popping and squealing and burning the hell up. That's how you handle rats."

Cobb scratched his head. "Look here, all this talk of rats frying brings back memories of my delightful Southern childhood."

"Watch out, fellas," West warned. "This Negro's about to let loose a tall one."

"No," Cobb protested, "this is good as gospel here. Consider my mouth a prayer book."

Lucius Monday pretended to back away. "I'm just making room for the lightning strike," he said with a grin.

"We ate 'em all the time," Cobb continued. "Used to go down to the river and knock up 'em upside the head. Shoot, man, you ain't had you nothin' until you've had some rat. Dip 'em in some flour, dust 'em with some salt and pepper, and drop 'em in some Crisco, you got yourself somethin'. Even better when you soak 'em in some buttermilk first. Stick to your ribs, I'm telling you."

"Now look who's talking John Brown jive," Reuben said.

Cobb acted like his feelings were hurt. "Hmph, last time I share a sentimental glimpse of my younger days with you hard-hearted burrheads. And some folks think you coloreds got merciful tendencies."

Reuben smiled. "Those are folks who've never seen me play checkers." He looked over at West. "I got you where I want you, my friend."

West stared at the checkerboard, puzzled. Reuben lifted a checker and plunked it down with a triumphant flourish. "Jump. Jump. Jump. And . . . jump!"

He swept up the rest of West's checkers and gathered them in his fist. "Savor the sour flavor of defeat, black man," he said. "I believe I shall keep my crown, thank you."

"Son of a gun," West hissed. "All this conversation threw me off my game."

"Man, the John Brown is getting deep in here," Reuben teased. "Cobb, you want a piece of me?"

Cobb's normally placid forehead suddenly wrinkled with concern. "Hold on," he said. "What is it, Talk?"

Talk Much had silenced the hi-fi and placed his palm on the front door. He stood patiently, waiting for enlightenment. Finally he pulled away. "Trouble's coming," he said. He retreated to his corner.

"Maybe we should call it a night," West said, but his suggestion was lost in the rude scream of police cruisers racing down Easton Avenue.

"Sounds like a whole squadron," Monday said, just as more hysterical sirens and squealing tires shattered the brief silence.

"Whoever they're after is probably halfway to Chicago by now—"

The door flew open. A slender, black-clad teenager dived through and crashed to the floor. Reuben recognized him immediately as one of the young Warriors of Freedom, Gabriel Patterson's ragtag "army." He had been handing out leaflets at Curly's funeral. On the lawn in front of Good Samaritan, he'd worn an expression of hard-won masculinity, an earnest gaze full of pride and fearlessness. Apparently he'd dropped his mask of courage somewhere during a night of endless ducking and dodging. Sprawled on the floor of the Black Swan, he merely looked tired and terrified, a boy hardly weaned from his mother's breast.

"What the hell?" George said.

"Please," whispered the young stranger.

"Close the door, Talk," Cobb said. "Let's get this boy some water."

"No time," the boy sputtered.

Reuben helped him to his feet. "What's your name, son?"

"PeeWee. PeeWee Jefferson. They've been hunting us. All night, they've been hunting us."

Monday thought he already knew the answer. They all did, he was sure. But he asked anyway: "Who? Who's been hunting you?"

"The police. They catch us, kick us around, then they let us go. They're bored."

George eyed the boy with undisguised skepticism. "Doesn't look like anything's broke on you," he said.

"Like I said, they're just kicking us around, scaring us half to death. 'We're keeping an eye on all of you,' they say. 'We know where you live. We know where your mama works.' Stuff like that."

"These crazy cops," Cobb said. "They're getting out of control."

"Getting?" George's narrow eyes blazed. "Somebody turns up dead seem like every goddamn day."

"One of them, he tries to make you sing."

All eyes were on the boy.

"What?"

"You heard me right. Going on and on about doo-wop. Got mad when I said I didn't know anything about it. He had me pinned on the sidewalk near the Top Hat Lounge. Said he'd shoot me if I couldn't do a song by the Ink Spots. But I got loose and I ran. Look, I appreciate your help, but I got to get out of here."

"Get out? You almost broke your neck trying to get in," Reuben reminded him.

Cobb moved to the front window. "Looks like they're going door to door," he said.

"Should we kill the lights?"

"No, Monday," Reuben said. "I think they'd notice." He turned to PeeWee. "Come with me," he urged. "Hurry."

Reuben and George led him toward the back of the shop. Reuben pointed to a pair of planks sitting atop an empty barrel. "I've been planning to do something with this. Guess now is as good a time as any." They pushed the barrel to the darkest recesses of the shop and helped PeeWee climb inside. "Don't make a sound," Reuben cautioned.

They replaced the planks, covered them with a stack of stretched canvases, and made it back to the checkers table just as the door swung open.

Detective Ray Mortimer sauntered in, accompanied by his stern black partner.

Reuben got up slowly, his hands in plain sight. "Evening, Detectives. Is there a problem?"

"Maybe," Mortimer said smugly.

"I'm Reuben Jones."

Detective Grimes gave no indication that he'd been to the Black Swan before. He regarded Reuben as coolly as a stranger. Perhaps according to some predetermined agreement, Mortimer was doing the talking.

"This your place, Reuben Jones?"

"Yes."

"What kind of business do you do here?"

"Like the sign says, this is a sign shop."

"Uh-huh. And Ananias Goode is a church deacon."

Reuben stole a look at Grimes. Not even a twitch.

"Awful late to be painting signs, ain't it?"

"It was a long day. We're relaxing before heading home. To our families."

"Relaxing. Imagine that."

Mortimer ordered the men to remain where they were. No strangers to interrogation, they didn't need to be told twice.

He studied each of them, returning again and again to Talk Much. Finally he spoke to him.

"Some reason you're so fond of that record player?"

Talk Much stared back implacably. "Trouble's coming," he replied.

Before Mortimer could respond, Reuben told him what he told everyone who encountered his strange colleague.

"That's Talk Much," he explained. "He doesn't talk much."

Mortimer shot an impatient look at Reuben. "Was I talking to you?"

Reuben considered his hands. He'd first gone to work at age eleven, hauling deliveries on his bicycle for a pharmacy. He'd been working ever since, lifeguarding, stacking ice, digging ditches, lifting freight—whatever it took to keep climbing. Once a freak wind blew his ladder from beneath him and he held on to a ledge three stories up, stayed alive by the grace of God and the strength of his grip. He took note of Mortimer's small, soft hands, each one dancing nervously at the edge of a hip. All things equal, Mortimer would go down easy. One hard punch to the jaw maybe, or an almost gentle twist of his pink neck. Reuben balled his hands into fists, stuffed them into his pockets to avoid thinking about them.

*M*ortimer kicked jars and cans, spilled brushes, knocked over easels, looked under tables. He unscrewed bottles and sniffed the contents. In sharp contrast, Grimes never moved his hands from his sides as he moved slowly toward the back of the shop. Watching him, Reuben remembered his way of taking in the whole room without noticeably turning his head. He was sure he would find PeeWee without breaking a sweat.

Mortimer remained fascinated with Talk Much. "Anybody ever tell you how much you look like Otis Redding? Spitting image, huh, Grimes?"

"Hush," the black cop commanded.

Mortimer reddened. He made a show of digging in his ears. "What's that? Because I thought I heard you sa——"

"Hush. I said hush."

Grimes stood transfixed. He had uncovered his daughter's portrait, to which Reuben had yet to apply the finishing touches.

"Fuck me," Mortimer said.

"Nothing here for you," Grimes said, gazing into his daughter's eyes. He kept his back to his partner. "Wait outside."

The white man trembled with anger. He started to protest but thought better of it and headed for the door. He paused and got in Reuben's face. Close enough to see his spittle landing on the sign painter's cheeks and nose.

"You think we're done here. But we're not."

Mortimer slammed the door, but Grimes never turned around. Although he stared at the portrait, his mind seemed far away, gone to some distant place and time. A tear slid down his face. Raising his black-gloved hand, he gently wiped it off. "How long?" he asked.

"Not long," said Reuben. "I'm nearly done."

Grimes nodded. Only then did he turn to face Reuben. "Tell the boy to wait here awhile."

He strode toward the door. Talk Much took a step in his direction. "Trouble's coming," he repeated.

The detective shook his head. "It's already here."

Doo-wop

*M*ortimer races through the North Side. His windows are down, but the rush of air fails to drown out the scents and sounds of the dark temptations surrounding him—the unavoidable funk and rhythm of life in this half of the city: the black streets, the black corners, the black skins shining in black windows and lounging insolently on black porches, where the smoky residue of hickory-smoked ribs still lingers. The loud voices, barking dogs, car horns, snatches of music, the distant wail of sirens.

As he bounces around, over and through the endless maze of potholes in front of Royal Packing Company, the stench of the day's slaughtered pigs does battle with the dark. Above him the blood-red moon seems more than appropriate. The evening's activities had provided the most fun he'd had in weeks, until his freak of a partner went creepy on him. First there was the incident in front of the Top Hat. Mortimer had been determined to make that boy sing some Ink Spots or pee in his pants, whichever came first. Kneeling beside the boy lying stretched out on the sidewalk, he sang softly, trying to lead his youthful captive into the first strains of "Cow Cow Boogie," but the idiot wouldn't go for it. Mortimer thought he was preparing to join in on the opening of "My Prayer," but he stayed stubborn. Then Grimes made a sound that distracted him, and the boy got away. Leaning into the little suspect's frightened, puzzled face, close enough to see his spittle landing on the monkey's cheeks and nose, he heard a noise behind his ear just like the click of a safety. When he turned around, Grimes's hands were at his sides and he was looking in the other direction. Tall and deadly silent, his black shadow revealed a hint of crimson under that bloody moon.

The second incident was at that peculiar-ass sign shop, the Black Swan. They'd cornered that sneaky little no-singing nigger when Grimes actually told him to shut up. Hush, he'd said. In front of other people.

"Spooky black-ass mother . . ." Mortimer finds himself pondering that awful click—had he only imagined it?

Loud as a gunshot, his rear windshield explodes.

"What the hell—"

He screeches to a stop at the curb, races out with his gun drawn. He wheels around frantically, scanning the darkness. He sees no one. In his car, a black rock, about the size of a fist, sits on the backseat.

I really don't need this, he thinks. Then again, maybe I do.

He gets back in his car, slowly cruises the neighborhood. Perhaps a little exercise would get it all out of his system. Make the rock thrower pay for his stupidity. Encourage him to sing a little doo-wop while he's at it. Between two buildings on West Belle, he thinks he spots a furtive movement, casually steers in that direction.

Nillmon, God rest his soul, he was a partner. Cover for you in a heartbeat, and never too busy or too chicken to bust a black ass when the occasion called for it. And that was nearly every day.

Of course he'd had other partners. None was as terrific as Nillmon, but none was as god-awful as the scary fucker he was stuck with these days. Always wearing black leather gloves in the heat of the goddamn day. Grimes could break a nigger just as good as a white cop could, but he was strangely choosy; not just any nigger would do. He'd shoot Mortimer a chilly stare to let him know certain niggers were hands-off.

A well-worn path leads behind the billboards. Mortimer, heading toward it as if on automatic pilot, recalls how it all went down. That crook Ananias Goode must have his wallet up somebody's ass. One day he's in there talking to the precinct captain, the next day my lieutenant's telling me some citizens' review board has filed a complaint against me. Coons kicking up dust, he says, you know how it is. Then the bastard assigns one of the two black detectives in the whole goddamn city to "partner" with me. Partner my ass. Spooky sonofabitch never even lets me drive.

Crossing Sarah Street, Mortimer loses himself in a fog of memories. So many ass kickings, all in the name of keeping the peace. The Hudson Brothers, Frank and Jesse, in the alley behind Beaumont High. That uppity L. B. Tate, thought he ran Hebert Street. Well, we took care of that. That blind nigger on Vandeventer. Nillmon had dropped dead of stomach cancer long before that. Drunk-ass Elrod Keys. He got stone-cold sober and started callin' for his mama when we stretched him across those railroad tracks. That headstrong fool named Alfonso. He was a nigger that needed a thorough job.

With one hand on the wheel Mortimer strokes the handle of his gun, now tucked into his belt. He leans out the window and spits harder than necessary.

Just past Sarah, he slows, cuts his engine. In the shadows a stone's toss away, he spies a figure cutting across a lot that is empty except for a pair of towering, improbably placed billboards. On one of them, a Champale ad features a grinning black couple dressed for a night on the town. The caption urges, "Ready . . . set . . . GLOW!" On the other, a white man beams despite his black eye. "Us Tareyton smokers would rather fight than switch," he declares. He and Mortimer would be the only white faces around if not for the South Side stragglers cruising nearby Washington Avenue—a.k.a. the Stroll— for black prostitutes. Mortimer's quarry disappears behind the beams supporting the billboards. A little foot pursuit will be good, prolong the pleasure of the hunt. Mortimer grabs his flashlight.

On a balcony two stories up, a window is open. Sounds of love ride the heat: faint jazz, the thump of a headboard against the wall, a woman moaning. To Mortimer it conjures fierce rutting—wild, sordid, beastly. He wants to stay and bask in its radiance. But he moves on. The Comet Theatre comes into view.

$\mathcal{T}$he moon is evil. Charlotte can't help thinking so.

It was superstitious talk, and Dr. Noel would never approve. But Dr. Noel probably also would not approve of a young lady walking unescorted through black Gateway's oldest neighborhood so long past nightfall. After checking on every last baby in the pediatric ward of Abram Higgins Hospital for the hundredth and final time, Dr. Noel would be cruising in her Cadillac to her mansion on Lindell Boulevard. Maybe she'd stop at Nat-Han Steakhouse and grab something good for a late dinner. Charlotte often imagined what the great woman did in the evenings after work. Charlotte's two years volunteering at Abram H. had changed her life. She'd seen her destiny in that fabled yellow-brick complex: She was born to be a healer. That feeling had only been reinforced by her time spent assisting the legendary Dr. Artinces Noel.

Dr. Noel was a nationally known crusader on behalf of

black babies. She had popularized a diet of bananas, rice, apple-sauce, and toast when a scourge of pediatric diarrhea threat-ened to wipe out the North Side's youngest. She'd fought loud, long, and hard for ice cream and bananas in the children's ward of Abram H. after finding out that white infants were being served all they could eat at the public hospital on the other side of town. A petite Southern lady with a brain for science and a will of steel, Dr. Noel had been featured in *Time, Life,* and *Ebony.* She could be impatient with adults, but she never hesi-tated to do everything humanly possible on behalf of children. As far as Charlotte was concerned, the good doctor walked on water. And she wanted to be just like her.

That's why she stayed, holding and rocking babies until the night nurses made her leave. Charlotte sings softly to herself and tries to ignore the moon. It's just a few blocks between Abram H. and the children's home. Ed had offered to walk her "home" several times, but she wasn't yet ready to share her life at the orphanage with him.

Taking the shortcut behind the billboards, she resolved to tell him everything one day soon. Then he'd understand why she had little stomach for his complaints about his meddling dad. What she wouldn't give for a meddling dad!

Hearing footsteps, Charlotte picks up speed. She's heard them on other evenings and thought nothing of it, but tonight, under a blood-burning moon, they've acquired a sinister ring.

$\mathcal{T}$he North Side never gets completely quiet. As for the South Side—what the white folks do when the sun goes down and they're tired but perhaps satiated from kicking the shit out of black folks all day long, Guts can only speculate. Most black people came to Gateway courtesy of the Great Migration. You'd never need to go back more than a generation, maybe two, to run up against a North Carolinian, a Georgian, or most likely, a Mississippian. Guts was an exception. Even his grandparents— on both sides—had been born and raised in Gateway. This is his city. It's in his blood, and though he can count the number of times he's been on the South Side on his two huge hands, he considers himself a metropolitan man. Times like these are among his favorites. His duties done, his woman waiting, he can roll through the streets taking his sweet time. Soaking in the sights and noises, the familiar, comforting blackness of his hometown. High rollers from Chicago and New York quickly grew bored and blew through like a storm. They said Gateway was a country city, barely "up south" from where the cotton grew high. And they were right. But that's precisely what Guts loves about it: It never gets too fast for comfort. If the Big Apple is the city that never sleeps, Gateway is the city that never woke all the way up. Easing his comfortable sedan west on Delmar with the river at his back, he takes comfort in his community's sleepy charms.

$\mathcal{D}$anger always has a scent, though most of us miss it. After the car crash, the drowning, the tragic stumble off the edge of the cliff, some witness will remark that they'd sensed it coming. But they'd written off that tickle in the nostril, that faint, rude hint of something foul, dismissed it as an allergy or a trick of the air. Charlotte knows better. Her life has left her sharp and sensitive, awake to any sign of atmospheric disturbance. In one foster house (she refuses to call them homes) after another, her nose for trouble has kept her out of it. She has learned to recognize the wispy, rotten fume that bypasses most of us. On the night of her twelfth birthday, it's what made her sit up in bed, waiting for the sounds that she knew would soon follow: the warning groan of a bedspring released from its heavy burden, feet sliding slyly into slippers that muffled the footfalls but not enough to entirely silence the creaking floorboard in the hallway outside her room. The scent led to the sounds that led to Charlotte's foster "father" easing open her well-oiled door with practiced stealth, only to encounter an empty bed and a wide-open window.

On this night, the scent follows the sound. Charlotte hears the footsteps long before the smell hits her. Perhaps it had been hidden in the beer fumes hovering in invisible clouds along Sarah Street, or lost in the teasing tang of hickory smoke from ribs long since consumed. When it hits her, acrid and insistent, she abruptly changes course.

*W*hen she turns, her profile is briefly exposed, the taut hips and firm breasts that Ed Jones has lovingly immortalized in charcoal. Mortimer takes in the curves, pleasantly surprised. Woman? Child? Woman enough. Like a disease bubbling up from a single injured cell, an idea forms.

*W*hen Guts gets his mind on Pearl, it seldom shakes free. Because she sashayed into his imagination back at the last stoplight, his attention is fixed. Up to that point, he had meditated on W. C. Handy, the way the streets look after a cleansing rain, the minor repairs he needed to make on the church van that he drives every Sunday. But then lovely Pearl wiggled her way into his neurons and synapses, and that was all she wrote. Guts can almost taste the meringue when a girl runs directly into the path of his sedan. He slams on the brakes, inches from her startled face. She turns and looks like she wants to say something, but thinks better of it and takes off.

"Why do people keep running in front of my car tonight? Can't a brother just go home and get some banana pudding and whatnot?"

Guts notices the air has changed. Something's messing with his meringue, and it's not the stench of Royal Packing Company. Unable to put his finger on it, he sighs, eases off the brakes.

Sweet nigger gals. To be around them all the time and not touch them was a frustration to Ray Mortimer. How different they were from black men, whom Mortimer despised more than he could say. The men looked all the same. The women, every one of them was distinct. They were so musical in their movements, the way their hips swung, the lilt of their voices. Of course he'd heard stories about them, had almost had sex with a black prostitute who was more than willing, but he'd lost his confidence ("C'mon, baby, let's see what you got," she'd said, but it sounded more like a challenge than an invitation). And now this little number, not a block from the Stroll. A veteran hunter, Mortimer is a cunning stalker of game. He knows this girl's plan to circle the Comet Theatre before she does. When she comes around the other side, breathing hard and half-blind with panic, he'll be waiting.

After nearly getting flattened by Guts's bumper, Charlotte resumes speed. Along the way she scans the ground for a bottle, a rock, anything. But it's too dark, and the stench of danger is so thick it clogs her lungs. Behind the Comet, she hesitates. Left? Right? She chooses, and the ground rushes up to meet her. It's a harsh landscape, pocked with pebbles and bits of broken glass that find the soft spots in her cheek. Something has hit her from behind. She fights, crawling and kicking. She is furious and swift but still a girl.

Mortimer places a hand over her mouth. "You scream and I will kill you," he says. Charlotte thinks of Ed, Dr. Noel, the babies in the ward. They are always so happy to see her.

She determines to roll over, to look the Devil in the eye.

As she flips onto her back, Mortimer flicks on his flashlight, the same instrument he used to knock her to the ground. Charlotte sees only the light, which quickly goes flying. Now she can make out only bright asterisks of color colliding with shadows. She hears sounds of struggle and the yelp of a man in tremendous pain.

And a voice.

"Run, girl. Get out of here and don't look back."

The words aren't shouted but still carry a certain effortless ferocity, as if the man who uttered them was accustomed to prompt obedience. Yet they are gentle at the same time, even kind. She'd never forget that voice. She gets to her feet, brushes the glass and pebbles from her cheek, and runs.

Danger reeks. Even Mortimer smells it now. The grip around his throat feels like steel. Suddenly it's gone, and Mortimer, flat on his back, seeks air, merciful air. He struggles to his knees. But now the flashlight is back and shining directly in his eyes. Beyond it is utter, ominous blackness.

"Wait," he pleads. It hurts to say it. "I'm a cop."

He reaches for his gun, but it's gone. He gropes for his badge.

Now Guts knows.

"Well, if it ain't Mr. Doo-wop. I'm a W. C. Handy man myself."

Mortimer is thrown flat on his back. He closes his eyes, but all he finds is more blackness. A boot, size 14 EEE, rests lightly on his throat.

"It's all about choices, my man. I could have chosen to head straight home to my banana pudding. I'm telling you, I could almost taste that meringue. But then that girl ran past my car and I decided to have myself a look-see. Come around here and find you trying to drag her down to your level. Choices, ya know? Tonight I stopped. Another day I might have kept on going. Who's to say how it all comes out in the end? Damned if you doo-wop, damned if you don't."

He puts his full weight behind his boot as Mortimer gurgles to an end.

Guts deeply appreciates his pun. Nothing new about that. Except this time he lets himself laugh.

A Virtuous Woman

*t*he first morning after Paul's disappearance, Rose began to reconsider. Maybe the mysterious stranger who dragged off her husband had been not an ogre but an angel instead. The Holy Spirit must have known that she was just a fractured jaw or stair-bumping tumble away from breaking all the way down, must have read her thoughts while she tended the bacon sizzling on her stove. God delivered Daniel, didn't He? Pulled Shadrach and his fellows from the fiery furnace? Maybe, just maybe, Rose Whittier, a humble servant, found herself next in line for a bit of heavenly grace. And didn't Rev. Josiah Banks just say on *Tent Meeting* what she'd heard all her days: He may not come when you want Him, but He always comes on time. She may have needed Him then even more than she realized. And now there she was. Sitting in the quiet with a song in her heart. At first she was ashamed of her joyous mood. But waking up without her usual burden was like lifting a window shade and letting the sun in. "Praise God," she said aloud.

On the second day, Rose washed all of Paul's clothes. She opened up her dryer, then thought better of it. Minutes later, Reuben Jones, standing in his kitchen and sipping from a cup of coffee, nearly burned himself with the steaming liquid. He motioned to Pristine, who joined him at the window. "Great Kooga Mooga," he said. "Do you see what I see?"

The couple watched in silent wonder as their next-door neighbor hung her husband's shirts on the line. They could tell by the subtle wobble of the clothespins dangling from her lips that she was probably singing as she worked.

That task completed, Rose scrubbed her already spotless toilet, tub, and sink. She scoured every pot and pan, swept and dusted every nook and corner. Lined up all the knives and forks. Tucked in the sheets with military crispness, just like Paul preferred them, then slept in a chair in the front room.

On the third day, she prayed. All day.

On the fourth day, she packed her bags. Later that day, she found herself on Pristine's porch. She poured her heart out to her neighbor, leaving out the specifics of Paul's exit and confirming only that he was gone, she hadn't heard from him, and she was glad.

Pristine just nodded as if she knew that moment would someday come. She made a few calls, and, within minutes, Rose had a job—office secretary at Good Samaritan—and another place to stay: the spare room at Mrs. Garnett's house. Her new hostess, smelling of Skin So Soft and sporting a blond dye job, clucked sympathetically after Reuben dropped Rose at her house. "Come right in, child," she said. "I know something about crazy husbands, so you don't have to tell me a thing. Unless, of course, you want to. Care for some lemon pie?"

On the fifth day, she dreamed of the handsome stranger with flake-gold eyes. In her dream, she was with Paul. They were leaving church when the man appeared in the aisle, blocking their path. The two men stared at each other.

Her husband frowned. "Problem?"

"No, brother," the stranger replied.

Paul snorted. "I'm not your brother."

On the sixth day, she was in the church office singing softly to herself while watering the plants.

"I'd know that voice anywhere."

"Oh, I didn't realize—" Rose turned and saw him. Bright eyes blazing in the afternoon sun.

"Stand still," he said. It was clear that he was talking to himself. "And consider the wondrous works of God."

Rose felt a warming sensation zoom straight from her toes to the top of her skull. She thought her head might take off and soar into space. Blushing, she wondered if he could see what she felt. He was staring so intently.

"You really shouldn't talk that way," she said when her voice returned.

"It's from Job."

"I *know* where it's from."

"Since when does a woman of the Word discourage a man from talking about it?"

"You talk about it, but do you believe it?"

"Every time I see you my faith is confirmed."

Nice. But Rose refused to smile.

"How did you—What are you doing here?" She was mad at herself for sounding so flustered.

"I live here. I might ask you the same."

Rose narrowed her eyes. "You live here."

"Did I stutter?"

"What do you mean you live here?"

"My work requires the good graces of men like Reverend Washington." He paused to let that sink in. "Plus, I'm a youth counselor at the church community center. I stay in the rectory."

"That doesn't sound like a long-term job."

Gabriel chuckled. She's interested, he thought, but trying not to let it show. "Reverend Washington wants me to work at the new boys' club going up. But I'm not so sure."

"You live in the rectory."

Gabriel shrugged. "Reverend Washington has his own home, and a wife. I've got no wife. I'm alone. *All* alone."

"Watch yourself, Mr. Patterson."

His smile was as dazzling as his eyes.

"So you remember my name."

*M*iles Washington's Sunday sermon was on virtuous women. He talked about Abigail, "a woman of good understanding and of a beautiful countenance" who was married to a man "who was churlish and evil in his doings." He went on to discuss Proverbs 31 in detail, warning his male listeners that any man who mistreated a woman would never "be known in the gates." He went on like he does, and Pristine, sitting next to Orville, Gloria, and Roderick in the third row, loved every minute. Casting her practiced eye over the saints, she easily noted the slender newcomer two pews over. He had been passing out leaflets the day of Curly's funeral.

Rev. Washington's typical homilies were mix-and-match blends of jazz, prophecy, celebration, and loving chastisement. He could take things as disparate as a bit of Scripture, a newspaper headline, and a snatch of overheard conversation, and turn them into something inspirational and memorable, a pulpit performance you could dance to or revel in, depending on how you felt. As he half-shouted, half-sang, the scar on his neck pulsed like a warning beacon. His regulars recognized the pulsing as a sign that he was getting revved up.

"More precious than rubies," he thundered. He was in full voice now. "Only *a fool* casts *a ruby* aside. Hah! Only *a fool* declines to cherish *a jewel*. Hah! I'm not talking about pimp clothes and shiny cars and pinkie rings. Hah! That means nothing—hah!—in the eyes of God—hah!—and shouldn't mean anything—hah!—to godly men. Are you *hearing* this?"

Pristine hardly missed her husband beside her. Getting Reuben to show up more than once a month was a dream she had all but given up on, and so the fault was hers. Like everything else, it came down to a matter of belief: "If ye have faith as a grain of mustard seed, ye shall say unto this mountain, Remove hence to yonder place; and it shall remove; and nothing shall be impossible unto you." Pristine knows the book of Matthew as well as anyone, but still.

Rev. Washington wasn't talking about Matthew or Proverbs 31 either. He had moved on to Psalm 82.

"It says in that psalm that we are all children of the most high. But that doesn't mean we should walk round with our heads in the clouds. Quite the opposite. It means, beloved, we must never fail to recognize God in ourselves and all around us. God is in all places and at all times, for all time. God is on the ground, beloved. Say that to your neighbor: God is on the ground."

The congregation obeyed, and Gabriel found himself exchanging the words with a friendly man sitting next to him. The man was with his wife, a sweet-looking woman in a clean, modest dress. In other times, full of withering contempt, Gabriel had dismissed such men as simpletons, unthinking dupes all too willing to buy into values that weren't even theirs. But there in the church, while the eloquent pastor sang his truth—"He who findeth a wife findeth a *good* thing, hah!"— all he felt for such men was envy.

Rev. Washington moved on to James 1:22—"Be ye doers of the word, and not hearers only, deceiving your own selves"—but what, Gabe asked himself, was *he* doing? Men like his church neighbor were quietly building families and communities—exactly what the Man didn't want them to do. Maybe they were the real revolutionaries.

Gabe's head was swimming. He stirred in his seat, craving air.

Then Rose began to sing. She stood in the choir loft, eyes closed, one hand on her breast. From her lips the sound flowed into something stirring, something profound. Gabriel was transfixed. Around him, others were captivated, transported, shaken. With tears silently falling down her cheeks, Pristine stood and waved her handkerchief. Gloria Bates got to her feet and began to dance in place until her hat fell off. They were among the first to feel it: The Spirit rose up and raced through the gathering of souls, raising the hairs on forearms and the backs of necks. Holiness hit in waves, taking hold of nearly all in its path. It began with a stomping of feet, the syncopated click of heels on the wooden floor. Soon the staccato stomp was punctuated here and there by a whoop, a cry, a ha-ha! Arms began to flap, hips swiveled, and hands thrust straight up in the air. Around and around God's children danced and shouted, shook sweat in every direction, elbows jutting at odd angles but striking no one. A collective moan seemed to emanate not from any human throat but from the air itself, an energy older than pain and stronger than time. And Rose's voice was all in it, thoroughly praising, summoning, raising the roof. Rev. Washington gripped the podium like a desperate lover and rocked his head back and forth so violently you feared for his life if you didn't know any better.

In time, the unfettered ecstasy gave way to a familiar,

reassuring stillness. The saints returned to their bodies. Rose's voice grew soft, then stopped. She opened her eyes and saw that the man with the flake-gold eyes was leaving the sanctuary.

*H*e returned later, popping up on Mrs. Garnett's front porch that same afternoon. "Claims he's here on church business," her skeptical hostess announced.

He was holding roses, but Rose pretended not to notice them.

"How did you find me?"

"I went door to door. All over the North Side."

"Stop lying."

"Oh, come on, don't be so harsh," he protested. "The North Side's only so big."

"For real. Tell me."

"Okay, Mrs. Garnett's in the church directory. I knew you were staying with her and, believe it or not, I also know how to read."

"Yet there's so much you don't know."

"The fear of the Lord is the beginning of knowledge," Gabriel said.

Rose frowned, or tried to. "You think you're charming, but you're going to get enough of mocking me."

Gabriel shook his head. "I'll never get enough of anything about you."

He stood as close to Rose as he dared, soaking up her aura so deeply that he lost track of time and missed a meeting of the Warriors—a meeting that he himself had scheduled. The phone in his room at the rectory went unanswered. At the community center, PeeWee and the others shared their fear that

Gabriel was losing interest in their cause. "This is some bull-shit," PeeWee said.

Gabriel and Rose sat on Mrs. Garnett's porch until evening, talking and punctuating their conversation with so much laughter that any passerby would have assumed they'd been lovers for a long and happy time. Finally they said nothing and found comfort in the quiet.

At first she wouldn't let him leave the flowers with her, but he made her promise to give them to Mrs. Garnett. Their fingers touched when he placed the bouquet in her hands, and a spark—electric and undeniable—passed between them. Gabriel looked to see if Rose felt it too. The expression on her face made it clear that she did.

"Nothing more to say tonight, is there?" Her lips were right there. But he didn't want to ruin his chances.

She looked away. "No, I guess not."

"Good night, Rose. Thank you for—Well, just thanks, that's all."

"Good night, Mr. Patterson."

Rose went inside and knelt by her bed. "Please, God," she said. "Send me a sign."

*T*he next day, when she had put away her final file, emptied out and washed the coffeepot, and straightened the papers on Rev. Washington's desk, it occurred to Rose that she needed some things from her old house. Against her best judgment, she asked Gabriel to accompany her. Just in case.

"Just in case what?" He seemed amused.

"In case he's up there and just hasn't been looking for me. In case he's up there with some other woman."

Rose knew Pristine would have alerted her to either of those scenarios, but she still wanted him to come.

Sullivan Avenue was still bright and quiet. Two doors over from Rose's old flat, a shirtless Mr. Collins was cutting his lawn with a rotary push mower. Across the street, Mrs. Cleveland was trimming her shrubs while a bottle of Coke sat nearby. Next door, Crispus was still breaking in his first baseman's mitt. Gabe, waiting outside for Rose, watched him toss a tennis ball against his front step. Without trying very hard, Gabe could see himself on a street like that, cutting his grass, playing catch with his son.

The ball rolled past the boy and over to Gabe. He tossed it back.

"Thanks," Crispus said.

"No problem. What's your name?"

"Crispus."

Gabe smiled. "Wow, like the revolutionary."

Crispus squinted up at the man. Although his eyes were hard to read in the glare of late afternoon, Crispus could tell they were the most unusual he'd seen besides Mr. Burk's. But they were different somehow, not like a zombie's at all.

"Not many folks know that."

"He gave his life for a cause," Gabriel said. "We should never forget him."

"What's *your* name?"

"Gabriel."

"Like the angel," Rose said.

Gabriel and Crisp turned and looked at her. Smiling, she held a shopping bag in either hand. Her expression told Gabriel that she was relieved, that she'd found nothing disturbing inside. He sensed that he was getting closer to her, easing past her sturdy defenses. He just needed to bide his time.

"Gabriel Patterson," he continued. "I work at the community center."

"And you're with the Warriors. I saw you in the paper."

Gabriel moved closer to Rose. "All is well, Mrs. Whittier?"

"All is well," Rose replied.

They walked off arm in arm, giggling slightly. Crispus, puzzled, stared after them.

The Justice Singers were the headliners at the community rally, but they were hardly the only acts on the bill. The rally was a fund-raiser for both the community center and the Coalition Against Police Brutality, for which Gabriel and Rev. Washington served as committee members.

Rose was blown away by the singers, a quartet consisting of two men and two women who were also frontline activists in various Southern campaigns. Rose loved the ease with which they turned gospel fervor into political urgency. Their capable harmonies made calls for action as right—and righteous—as calls to the altar.

She also enjoyed seeing Gabriel in such a public light. He shared emcee duties with Rev. Washington and was nearly his equal. He came off as angry but committed, and appeared frustrated when the crowd's solid intensity didn't seem to match his own. He reminded his listeners that patience could easily decline into dangerous passivity. "We can't afford to let outsiders feel as if they can come into our communities and trample our children," he warned. "Trample our rights, trample our lives." Pigs who tried, he said, would do so at their own risk.

Afterward, Gabriel introduced Rose to the Justice Singers. He asked the group's lead tenor if they had any plans to expand.

"We've been singing together for a few years now," he replied. "We like the sound we have. But there need to be justice singers everywhere, don't you think?"

"*That's* you, Rose. Gateway City's very own justice singer."

They were on the steps of the church, still winding down from the rally's fever pitch.

Rose smiled. "Look who's talking. You're pretty good at moving the people yourself."

"But it takes time, paragraphs and paragraphs of words. You can do it in a single note."

Rose remembered Curly's funeral, her first public performance in years. Rev. Washington had persuaded her to do it, and Paul had figured he had too much to lose if he denied her. She'd had the crowd as soon as she opened her mouth. And last Sunday? That had been her best singing ever. And the most satisfying part about it was how easy it had been. She took a breath and the Spirit took over.

They left the church and headed toward Mrs. Garnett's.

"You were pretty hard on Reverend King," Rose said.

"Not too hard, I hope. I respect the man."

"I couldn't always tell."

"I'm just wary of making our movement about just one man. I suspect that's what the oppressors want. Cut off the head and the body dies."

"That's an ugly image."

"The truth is that way sometime."

They walked in silence.

"Look," Gabriel explained. "All I'm saying is nonviolence

clearly has its limits. Is that what we make babies for? To give them up to our enemies?"

"Something tells me you don't have much experience with violence," Rose said. "How truly awful it is."

Unconsciously, she touched her loose molar with the tip of her tongue.

"So we just keep turning the other cheek. Rose, I'm more of an Old Testament kind of brother. You know." Gabriel lowered his timbre dramatically, as if speaking in the voice of God. "I will wipe Jerusalem as a man wipeth a dish, wiping it, and turning it upside down."

Rose clucked. "Mocking me again."

Gabriel grinned brightly. "Just having a laugh is all. He that is of a merry heart hath a continual feast."

Suddenly growing serious, he stopped and held Rose by her shoulders. "Listen. Please don't take this the wrong way. And please don't jump up and run after I say what I have to say. When I was talking about babies earlier, I wasn't just talking about children in general. I actually was being quite specific."

"I don't follow."

"I had a vision. I'm not a man given to visions, mind you. But I heard you before I ever saw your face. And then, when you walked down the steps of the church, a vision of the future overcame me. I saw my children yet unborn—"

"Enough, Gabriel. Stop right now."

"Don't you believe in visions, Rose?"

"I believe you don't know anything about me. Or maybe you're not hearing me. And you keep trying to get me to forget that I'm married."

"Not even a kiss, then?"

"Not even that."

"But—"

Rose put her finger to his lips. For them it was an extraordinarily intimate gesture. Neither of them breathed, letting the contact linger. With great effort, she pulled away.

"Do you want me to start calling you Mr. Patterson again?"

"Rose, you're torturing me."

"At least I'm not lying to you. I feel what you feel. But I do things the right way."

"I'm sick of Paul."

"He's my husband. He might be—"

"Churlish and evil?"

"I was going to say he might be absent but he's still my husband. I made a vow."

Gabriel had put out feelers regarding Paul's whereabouts but had come up with nothing. He'd vanished just like Detective Mortimer. Gabriel said nothing to Rose, but he wouldn't have been surprised if there was a connection between the two disappearances. Not that he would waste a single breath looking for one. Although it would be good to know where that fool Whittier was. They needed to talk man to man.

*T*he tension had deflated by the time they reached Mrs. Garnett's house. Rose had even allowed Gabriel to buy her a cone when they passed by Horack's Dairy. Little by little, he began to tell her about his childhood, about his hopes and dreams.

"I'm not saying I've ever wanted a picket fence and all of that. Just a little space like my dad and I had. We only had a front stoop really, no yard, but we made it work. I worry that

I'll never be the man my dad was. Compared to his, my hands are like pudding. He had palms like leather, and those thick, nicotine-stained nails that looked strong enough to pull up railroad spikes."

Rose watched Gabriel closely. He often spoke candidly about the desire he claimed to feel for her. But he seldom had much to say about what he'd experienced or where he'd been.

"Like I say, all I need is just enough to do right by mine. Enough to make sure little Marie has everything she needs. But sometimes the struggle—"

"What did you say?"

"Hmm? I was talking about picket fences."

"No, after that. What did you say?"

"I want to make sure Marie has every—"

"Who's that? Who's Marie?"

Gabriel smiled shyly. "That's what I'm going to call my daughter."

"How did you come up with that?"

"It was my mother's name. After she died, my dad talked about her all the time. Hardly ever talked about anything else. But he didn't like to say her name. He always said, 'Your mother this, your mother that.' Whenever he slipped and said 'Marie,' his voice would break and his eyes would fill with tears. After a while he stopped slipping. And I learned to miss hearing my mother's name. I said to myself, 'I know how to fix that. Someday.' "

He turned to her. Her face was tilted upward in amazement. She grabbed his arm.

"Are you trying to tell me you don't like that name?"

"Gabriel Patterson, pray with me."

"Huh?"

"You heard me. Pray with me, right now."

They knelt by the side of the road.

$\mathcal{L}$ater Rose prayed again, alone.

"Okay, Lord, you've given me a sign," she said. "Now I need a way."

Ashes to Ashes

1928

Octavius "O.G." Givens was relieving himself when the trouble began. He had ambled into Lemon's Woods behind the barbecue party, his mind on unloading his bladder, burdened as it was with homemade white lightning. He was a young man, just sixteen, but at two hundred–plus pounds and a whisker shy of six feet, he could pull his own weight with strength to spare. The son of a murdered moonshiner, he'd taken over his daddy's still and done well enough to keep his mama in biscuits and himself in brogans—the shiniest available in Liberty.

O.G. didn't just spit and swagger like a man. More than one grown gal had sworn to her sisters that those big hands of his were useful for plenty besides bare-knuckle brawling and squeezing cane. Word was he could stroke a woman until she hollered "Lawd, ha' mercy!" All of that before he got down to the real business of plowing that furrow like a natural-born farmer.

The barbecue wasn't a church event. Otherwise he'd have left his best hooch at home and relied on his trademark lemonade. Already half-unzipped, he tossed a wholehearted invitation over his shoulder to the Redd twins as he entered the trees and prepared to do his business. He had just shaken off the last drops when he heard a giggle. He looked and saw Annie Mae Redd, the more outgoing of the twins, sashaying eagerly in his direction.

"So you decided to join me after all," he said with a confident grin.

She answered with a compliant squeak.

Odder even than O.G.'s precocious success was his friendship with Leo "Mile-a-Minute" Madison. The fastest Negro in Liberty, Leo was as devout as O.G. was dirty. As a young boy, he'd seen the Son of God in a cotton field. Later that evening, the folks in the quarters asked him to describe the experience. "It was like looking into a mirror," he said. "That's the only way I can describe it." Since then he'd been convinced that his steps were guided.

The reverend and the rascal, as they had been fondly known since they were knee-high to saw grass, had been closer than brothers from the get-go. They remained inseparable even as they stared down advancing adulthood, which for most Negro men in Liberty meant an endless term of backbreaking labor in the blistering fields or a short, dirty life wrestled to a violent end in a turpentine camp. Leo and O.G. meant to avoid all that, Leo by living the life of Christ and O.G. by living a life of crime. They pursued their respective paths with admirable discipline, thick as thieves all the while.

The day that changed their lives forever proceeded typically enough, with the young reverend-to-be in town praying over the sick while his pal O.G. bounced up and down between Annie Mae's experienced, willing thighs. So enthusiastic were her squeals and sighs that they drowned out the drama unfolding nearby.

"Well, well, Bufe," said Bob Stone, "looks like we found ourselves a party."

Just like that, the happy hubbub of jug, fiddle, and harmonica, the rib eating and backslapping, came to an abrupt and unwanted end.

"Uh-huh, a party," said Buford, Bob's idiot friend. Snot was running down his chin.

"We're just having a barbecue, Mr. Stone. Minding our own business." That was J. C. Frison, an able hand at the sawmill that Bob Stone's father owned. The corded veins on J.C.'s forearms were nearly as big as Bob's sunburned neck.

Bob guffawed. "Business? Now that's a funny notion, Nigras having business. Only businesses round here are owned by my daddy or his friends. That means one day alla y'all will work for me. Might as well start now. Somebody pull me up a chair."

While someone dragged a folding chair forward, others began gathering plates and wrapping up dishes.

"Wait just a minute," Bob commanded. "Before y'all hightail it out of here, I want to sample your fixin's. Those look like ribs. Buford, nobody cooks ribs like Nigras. I know because I growed up on 'em. Bring us both a plate, and I want first-class service."

Bob stroked his chin and eyed the women. "Rita Mae, you come wait on Buford." Rita Mae, the less outgoing of the Redd twins, came forward reluctantly, carrying a plate.

"J.C., get us one of those card tables and a couple lemonades. Set us up right."

When Bob's instructions had been carried out, he rested his eyes on Floretha Madison, a coal black beauty much older than he. In fact, she was Leo's mama. Neither time nor its ravages had left any visible mark upon her lithe figure and unlined face. Despite her comeliness, Miss Floretha, a widow, was treated in the quarters with the deference and courtesy elders used to be able to reasonably expect. Bob Stone was not from the quarters.

"Floretha, I do believe I choose you," he said, licking his lips.

"Hold on, Mr. Stone," said J.C. "We don't want any trouble."

"That's right," Bob said. He never took his eyes off Miss Floretha. "And there won't be any because you're gonna sit your black ass down right there on the ground. All of you boys do that, before you get any stupid ideas and find yourselves out of jobs tomorrow."

Sullen and humiliated, the half dozen or so men at the barbecue shuffled forward and sat on the ground. Rage rose from them as thick and redolent as the smoke that had issued from the barbecue grills not long before. Unlike the smoke, which rode the air over the woods and on to far more pleasant places, their anger had nowhere to go. So they sucked it up and held it inside, where the only damage would be to themselves. Unable to face their tormentors, their women, or each other, they stared at the dirt.

Miss Floretha sat on Bob's lap as instructed. Trembling but maintaining her dignity, she held his glass of lemonade to his lips after he sloppily tore into each rib. She spoke softly while he sipped.

"Now, Mr. Stone," she whispered. "I've known your family since before you was born. We've always gotten along." Her tone was gentle, motherly. "We sure do appreciate your visit, but we've got work to do for you tomorrow. If we don't go home soon, say our prayers and get our rest, we won't be any good for you. So why don't you and Buford just let us go on home? Hmm? Just let us go on home."

But it was to no avail. Bob elbowed Miss Floretha off his

lap. "Bufe, will you look at this? I've gone and got sauce on my hands. Hard to eat ribs without your fingers getting sticky."

"I'll get you a napkin," Miss Floretha said.

"No need. No need at all. I've got something funner in mind. Bend over."

A silent second stretched into a long painful minute. Or so it seemed.

Miss Floretha prayed that she'd misheard. "Beg your pardon?"

Bob snorted. "No need to beg for what's given freely. Bend your pretty self right on over."

A groan escaped from one of the men. A woman began praying softly.

"Don't like what you see, look away," Bob shouted.

"Please, Mr. Stone," Miss Floretha said, still whispering. "Why are you doing this?"

"Because I'm bored, and maybe a little bit drunk too. Now bend."

Miss Floretha bent from the waist, resting her hands on her knees. Delicately as a maiden adjusting her petticoats, Bob lifted the back of her dress and folded it neatly above her hips.

"All I want to do is wipe my hands, that's all," Bob said. "Can't a gentleman just wipe his hands?"

He mashed his palm against Miss Floretha's rear, smearing her underpants with sauce. "Bufe, when I'm done, you need to wipe your hands too."

O.G. sauntered out of the woods, adjusted his pants, and let loose a satisfying belch. Then he looked up and saw Bob Stone with his hands on his best friend's mama. He unbuckled his belt before he took another step.

"Rita Mae, Annie Mae—whoever the hell you are—get up and get your black ass in position. Bufe's got a lot of sauce on his hands. Hell, Bufe, you might want to wipe some of that snot off while you're at it."

"I'll whip you like a nigger."

Bob Stone looked up and saw O. G. Givens standing in front of him and breathing fire, his belt coiled in his fist like a rawhide snake.

Bob slowly and stiffly rolled his head on his shoulders, as if struggling with the effects of a hangover. Suddenly deadly sober, he glared at O.G.

"You ready to die, boy?"

"Right here, dyin' gets done two ways," O.G. said. He turned to his friend's mother.

"Get up, Miss Floretha. You too, Rita Mae."

The women complied and were quickly hustled away by their friends.

Bob stood up and wiped the rest of the sauce on his shirt-tail. "We know where you live, Ock. Tavius." He said it like he was spitting a bad taste out of his mouth.

"Ain't but one place I call home."

After Bob and Buford slunk away, the gathering returned to life. But partying was the last thing on their minds.

"We got to get you out of town, O.G."

"They're sure to come around nightfall."

"We'll stand with you, O."

O.G. grunted and pulled on his belt. "Like you stood with me just now? Don't y'all worry about it. Y'all have to work for that man's family. I don't."

Annie Mae grabbed his hand. "What are you gonna do?"

"Going back to my place. I'll wait for them there."

"They'll kill you, O.G."

He grabbed her and kissed her hard. Maybe it would be the last time he felt such softness.

"My daddy wouldn't live under any man's heel," he said. "Neither will I."

Leo had always been too clever to let a white boy talk him into a footrace, so his speed was known only on the dark side of the tracks. White folks knew him as Leo, or Floretha's Boy.

Any Negro who saw him that night would not have been amazed to spy him tearing through the fields like a black blur. It had been almost sundown when word had reached him all the way in town, and he had taken off almost immediately, burning up the rough tracks and hidden trails away from the beaten paths where white men traveled. He knew the wild country as well as anyone, thanks to his half-Seminole grandpa. The old man had taught him how to string a bow and stalk game. Together they brought down everything from deer to squirrel, always sharing their haul with O.G. and his family.

As a red moon rose and dropped a haze of sinister crimson over the surrounding darkness, Leo prayed that his shortcut would lead him to O.G.'s shack before the mob got there. If it didn't, he knew that his friend would die without begging, without showing the least sign of fear.

But there was no mob. Perhaps emboldened by drink or an inflated sense of their own power, Bob and Buford hunted their quarry alone and on foot. It was true: they had to be two of the dumbest white men in the whole South. Leo's path through the woods enabled him to intercept them nearly a mile from their destination. He walked toward them slowly, waving his white shirt above his head.

"What the hell?" Bob squinted into the darkness.

"It's that saved nigger," Buford said. He was holding a bottle and smelled like beer. Snot was running down his chin.

"Please," Leo said. "You don't want to do this." Bob appeared to have a handgun tucked into his waistband. Leo could spot no weapon on Buford.

"You trying to tell white men what they can and cannot do?"

"No, Mr. Stone. All I'm saying is let's think for a minute. It was my mother you insulted. Deal with me. I'm not trying to fight you."

"You're usually a sensible nigger," Bob said, "not like the one we're goin' to see. Wait a minute. Did you say *insulted*? I gave your mother the time of her life. Hell, I expect she'll be coming from the quarters any minute now, beggin' me for more."

Quick as a cat, Leo pinned Bob to the ground. Almost as quickly, Buford smashed his bottle across Leo's neck. He wiped his nose with the back of his wrist.

Leo felt a sharp, slashing pain and rolled onto his back. Bob struggled to his feet, breathing heavily. "Want to get yourself gutted tonight?"

"Yeah," Buford said. "We can kill two niggers just as easy as one."

"Just let him bleed out," Bob instructed. "If he lives it'll be a lesson to him."

Leo woke up dazed. The red moon above slowly glowed into focus. Remembering the fight, he put his hand to his neck. It came away wet. He crawled to his feet, holding his shirt to the wound. After stumbling back into the woods, he washed his neck in a shallow pool and packed the long, ugly cut with mud. Then he headed to his friend's home. Staggering, he came to O.G.'s still at the edge of the woods, a short distance from his shack in the little clearing. The two friends had spent many a night together in those woods, laughing, arguing, planning for a future that made room for real men. Real men like Leo's grandfather, who taught him that any hunter worth his salt was never far from his weapons. Keeping low to the ground, he turned left, walked ten paces to a hollow tree, and reached inside. Without looking, he quietly gathered his bow. Listening hard for sounds of activity at the shack, he strapped on his quiver.

He peered between two branches, where the red moon shone on O.G., beaten and bruised. Leo suspected he'd been shot and pistol-whipped. His arms were bound, and he was kneeling in front of a stump. His pants were around his ankles. His penis was curled on top of the stump. In front of him, Bob Stone had a small fire going. He dipped a knife in and out of the flames while Buford prepared to pee nearby.

"Gon' whip my ass, huh, nigger? Who's doing the whippin' now?"

Bob was raging. O.G. wasn't gagged but said nothing, determined to go out like a man.

"My glory was fresh in me," Leo prayed, "and my bow was renewed in my hand." He notched the first arrow.

Buford's water leaked out of him as if he was still alive. It trickled steadily to the ground as if he were still breathing and had not died standing up, with an arrow through his throat. His windpipe severed, he couldn't even gasp. Finally he tipped over, and made an ugly sound when he landed. Snot dripped down his chin.

Bob heard the sound and turned. He stood, just what Leo had prayed for, and took an arrow through the heart.

Minutes later, the reverend and the rascal were dragging two bodies into the still. "You okay?" the reverend asked.

"Yeah, flesh wound," the rascal replied.

Leo pulled a length of burning wood from the fire and prepared to touch it to the still. "Ashes to ashes," he said. "Shall we pray?"

"No, nigger, let's *run*," O.G. replied. "Then we'll pray."

No black man killed a white man in Dixie and survived. Under cover of darkness and with the help of others who'd followed the same blood-streaked path of the Great Migration, Leo and O.G. fled the South. As did many before them, they shed their old names to throw any pursuers off their trail.

1968

Now, decades later, Rev. Miles Washington and Ananias Goode were helping dispose of another white man's body. Minutes before, they had reclined in the luxurious backseat of Goode's sedan as Guts Tolliver expertly steered it toward the twin gates behind Harry Truman Boys' Club. Detective Grimes pulled up, unlocked the gates, and waved them through. Guts leaned on the gas. Soon the acreage on which they stood would be turned into ball fields and playgrounds, but at the moment it was fallow ground. Ananias lit up a fat cigar.

"How's the secretary working out?"

"Rose? She's a peach."

Twin beams of light streamed briefly on the field, then shut off. An engine was killed, a door opened, and the undertaker stepped out. "Got him right here," Mr. Burk said. "Nice and cold."

Guts went in back of the hearse, slid the body out, and tossed it over his shoulder. It was wrapped in a body bag. The men followed Rev. Washington through an opening in the rear of the club. They paused before a huge crater. "Dump him here," the reverend said.

With a simple shrug, Guts tossed the last of Detective Mortimer into the pit. Burk followed with a bag of quicklime.

"They pour the cement for the pool tomorrow," the reverend said.

"Good deal," said Ananias. "Ready to roll?"

"No, we should pray first."

"You're not serious," the gangster protested.

He looked around. Guts took off his hat and held it over his heart. Burk bowed his head. The reverend cleared his throat.

The gangster sighed. "You *are* serious," he said. He bowed his head.

"Heavenly Father," the reverend said. "Forgive us our trespasses as we dispatch this sinner to the fires of eternal torment."

"Amen."

"Amen."

"Amen."

"A-muthafuckin'-men." Ananias looked around, embarrassed. "Sorry," he added.

They headed back to the field.

Burk turned to the others. "Poker Tuesday?"

Ananias nodded. "Yep."

"See you then." He started up his hearse.

The gangster's cigar had shriveled into a chewed-up stump. He flicked it to the ground.

Guts turned to him, hat still in hand. "Boss," he said, "about this." He nodded toward the pit.

"Don't sweat it," Ananias said. "It was going to happen. Just a question of when."

Grand Opening

*A*bove the bones of Detective Ray Mortimer, flashbulbs popped.

Grandly waving his hand across the gleaming expanse of black-and-white tile, Rev. Miles Washington smiled for the cameras. "This will be the only Olympic-size pool on the entire North Side," he declared. "When the streets get too hot, this will be the place to cool off."

At the grand opening of Harry Truman Boys' Club, Rev. Washington led a tight parade of media and dignitaries through the huge complex, pointing out its various features. His group included news crews from two TV stations, a pair of aldermen, fellow members of the clergy, a local sports celebrity, Ananias Goode, and Guts Tolliver, who despite his girth was nimble enough to stay out of camera range. Starting at the opposite end of the facility, Gabriel Patterson, who seemed to be the minister's new protégé, led a series of informal rambles for groups composed mostly of anonymous folks from the neighborhood. Large welcome banners, created by the men of the Black Swan, draped over doorways and wound around staircases. The hallways gleamed, and the floors gave off the faintly chemical scent of pine cleaner.

Walking with his family in one of the Patterson groups, Crispus ran into Polly Garnett on the upper level near a glass wall overlooking the pool. Under the watchful eye of his parents, he played it cool.

Polly didn't do cool. Like her mother, she was a warm-blooded creature.

"They need a girls' club too, don't you think?"

"I suppose," Crispus glumly replied.

"You know they're having refreshments downstairs, right? My mommy made—"

"Yes, yes, lemon pie, I know."

Polly put her hands on her hips and rolled her neck. "What's your malfunction?"

"Nothing. I'm fine." Crispus couldn't believe Polly's nerve, just stepping up to him as if everything was uptight. Could she really have forgotten the awful way she'd toyed with his affections?

Polly kept right on chattering, and Crispus finally gave in to her insistent charm.

Soon they were giggling and having a ball.

A few feet away, Reuben had his arm around Pristine. He rubbed her shoulder playfully. "Takes you back to the Pine Street Y, doesn't it?"

Pristine laughed. "Not exactly. Looks like you can fit two or three Pine Streets in that and have room left over."

"Oh, come on," Reuben said. "Pine Street had plenty of room. And this pool isn't so big. It doesn't even have a high board."

"That's because it's for kids," Pristine explained. "And you know how some boys are." Her voice betrayed a hint of mischief. "They're liable to jump off something high to impress somebody. Sometimes they get hurt that way."

"Not if they're anything like me," Reuben said. "I used to do somersaults like one of those cliff divers on *Wide World of Sports*."

"They'd better hurry up and put some water in that pool," Pristine said. "Before it gets filled with John Brown jive."

"That's a big pool," Polly said to Crispus. "Can you swim?"

"Not yet. But my mom said I can come here for lessons. I can't go fishing again until I do."

"Why did she say that?"

"Because I fell in the lake at Fairgrounds Park and almost drowned. My dad had to pull me out."

"I'm glad he did." They smiled at each other awkwardly. Crispus was beginning to think again about a long-term relationship. You never know, he thought. I just might do Curly proud.

"I already know how to swim because I was in Tiny Tots at the Y."

"Really? I almost did Tiny Tots, but that trampoline . . . Let's just say that jumping on the bed is adventure enough for me."

"Do you think he can swim?"

Crispus looked around. "Who?"

"You know who. That boy on your couch."

If there had been water, Crispus might have thrown himself through the window and hurtled headfirst toward the deep. Instead he sighed, pretended that Shom was calling him, and excused himself.

"Right," Polly said, watching his retreating back. "I may be beautiful but that don't mean I'm stupid."

In truth, Shom wasn't even present. The Roadrunners were in a spring tournament at Forest Park. Reuben hoped to get there before the third inning.

Downstairs, standing in line with Charlotte for the free

cups of cola donated by the Vess Soda Company, Ed wasn't having much more luck than his little brother. Charlotte had been
distant lately. She had skipped nearly a week of school, then
returned bearing traces of mysterious bruises that she didn't
care to explain. Ed began to wonder about an abusive father or,
worse, a romantic rival.

By the grand opening, she was just about back to her usual
bossy self. "Just promise me you'll go."

Ed ran his fingers through his hair. Since ditching the Murray's pomade and stocking cap, he couldn't stop caressing the
abundant wool sprouting atop his scalp. It was as if he wanted
to reassure himself that the waves were gone for good.

"You're keeping secrets from me and you want me to make
promises to you?"

Charlotte folded her slim arms in front of her.

"It's for the best."

"How come I can't call you?"

"I told you. I have a curfew."

"How come I can't walk you home?"

"You do."

"I mean *all the way* home."

Charlotte took Ed's hand. "All of this is beside the point.
I'm just asking you to go see the man, what do you have to lose.
Promise?"

"Charlotte."

"Charlotte nothing. Promise?"

"I promise to think about it."

She rubbed her thumb across his knuckles. "Well, at least
that's a start."

They grabbed their cups and moved aside to make space
for the VIPs entering the room. Among them, Charlotte
noticed a running back for the local NFL team. Like Ed, he'd

begun to grow his hair out. "Wonder how he's going to get all that under a helmet," she said.

"It won't be easy, that's for sure."

That voice. Charlotte turned and studied the ample visage of Guts Tolliver. They stared at each other. He had been her rescuer. Of that she was certain. "You were—"

Guts put his massive finger to his lips and gently shook his head.

Ed watched this exchange with curiosity and a growing anger. Recognizing Guts and taking note of the way he seemed to swell to fit the room, he realized his anger had nowhere to go. The giant assassin looked down on Ed with good-natured amusement.

He tipped his hat. "That's a good girl you got," he said. "Look out for her."

Ed nodded, trying to look unconcerned even though he'd developed a sudden urge to go to the bathroom.

"And don't worry," Guts added. "She only has eyes for you."

"How does he know that?" Ed asked as they headed to the gymnasium. They sat on the floor with their backs to the wall.

"It's complicated," Charlotte said. Ed waited, but she had nothing more to say.

Across the gym, the Young Hearts singing group occupied one corner, where they loudly made a mess of a Temptations medley. The backing band wasn't much better. The drums and the bass seemed to be arguing with each other, and the dispute threatened to burst right through the wall.

In another corner, Rose helped Mrs. Garnett tend the refreshment table. They nearly had to shout in order to hear themselves over the music.

"March came in like a lamb and it's going out the same

way," Mrs. Garnett said. She sliced pie with the easy grace of a woman who knows her way around the kitchen.

Rose, setting out paper plates in neat array, agreed. "Hasn't this been a beautiful spring? And it's only going to get better."

"I don't know, April's coming up."

"What's wrong with April?"

Mrs. Garnett paused and took a sip of Vess cola. The throbbing music made the liquid shake in her cup long after she set it back down. "You know what they say. It's the cruelest month."

Rose handed a plate and a spoon to a woman who approached their table. The woman thanked them and smiled shyly. "I've heard you sing in church. You sound lovely," she said.

"Thank you kindly," Rose said.

"Your husband must be very proud. In fact, I know he is."

Rose frowned. "And how would you know that?"

The woman took a step back. "I meant no offense. It's just that he told me so himself. He was bragging on you."

Rose was standing now. "My husband was bragging on me, you say. When was this?"

The woman was looking at Rose as if she had a duck on her head. "Why, just now," she replied, visibly losing confidence. "While he was taking us on the tour. He said be sure to stop by the gymnasium to get some of Mrs. Garnett's delicious lemon pie and say hello to his bride."

"The tour," Rose said. She was beginning to get the picture.

Mrs. Garnett had already gotten it. She suppressed a giggle. "Her husband's like that," she told the woman. "He's on the boastful side."

The woman smiled and moved on, relieved but not entirely sure why.

Rose looked at Mrs. Garnett in amazement. "That Gabriel Patterson. When will he learn?"

Mrs. Garnett stared back at her. "I imagine he's wondering the same thing about you."

"*Anyway,*" Rose said, "you were telling me about April."

"Right. It's supposed to be cruel. And it will be here the day after tomorrow."

"Who says it's cruel?"

"I can't say for sure, but I know he was talking about April."

"Well, whoever he is, I hope he's wrong. I for one have had enough of cruelty. I only want to hear about love."

"That makes two of us, sister."

The women raised their cups of Vess cola and gently touched them together.

"To love," they said.

"Excuse me, ladies."

Mrs. Garnett looked up to see a tall, dark-skinned man with a brilliant white beard. It had been trimmed to geometrical precision, perfectly framing a pair of generous, sensual lips. The man's eyes managed to be fierce and friendly at the same time, and they twinkled as he spoke.

"My, our table is popular today," Mrs. Garnett said, nervously straightening her dress. "How can I help you, kind sir?"

He leaned forward. "You can start by telling me if you made this pie."

Mrs. Garnett inhaled his scent, a masculine blend of Skin Bracer and menthol cigarettes. "I did make it. Do you like it?"

The man chuckled. He had a deep, rumbling laugh that Mrs. Garnett decided she liked as much as his smell. "Like it? I thought I had died and gone to heaven. I believe I could eat this pie every day for the rest of my life."

"Would you like for me to tell you how I make it?"

"I'd like you to tell me whatever you please. My name's Monday. Lucius Monday." He offered his hand.

Mrs. Garnett reached out and took it. "I'm Mrs. Garnett," she said. "The recently divorced Mrs. Garnett."

She leaned over and put her lips close to Rose's ear. "March can go ahead and go out like a lion, if you ask me. I ain't got nothing against lions."

She winked, stood up, and took her new suitor's hand.

"Let's start with the filling," she began. "You don't want it to be too sweet."

The man smiled as they moved away. "Not too sweet. Got it."

"Right," Mrs. Garnett cooed. "Because it's got to be tangy too."

The long day wound down. The VIPs lingered just enough to pose for a few pictures and make sure their names got mentioned in the appropriate columns, then beat an unceremonious retreat. The Jones family left in time to see Shom hit a home run from each side of the plate. Ed secured a quick cuddle from Charlotte before working the late shift at SuperMart.

Someone talked some sense into the Young Hearts and they switched to a round of ballads. In the middle of the gym floor, Mrs. Garnett danced with her new beau. She whispered and giggled like a young girl as she glided in her stockinged feet, her shoes dangling from one dainty hand. Polly watched in sullen silence until Rose told her to help her clean up. Rose, gathering the unused plates and spoons, looked up to see that Orville and Gloria were also on the floor, dancing cheek to cheek. Orville was leaving his high school post to become director of education at Harry Truman. He and Gloria had announced a June wedding. Roderick—"the North Side's homegrown genius" was how Rev. Washington had described him to the press—planned to offer tutoring as part of Harry Truman's after-school program.

"In the spring, a young man's fancy lightly turns to thoughts of love."

Rose turned away from the dance floor to see Gabriel standing beside her.

"I don't know if you should be talking to me about such things," she said. "Seeing as how you have a wife and all."

"What wife?"

"The one you've been bragging about while you conduct your tours. Don't think I haven't heard."

"Oh, her," Gabriel said. "She's not really my wife, although she wants to be. Since I can't marry her, I thought the least I could do was give her a dance."

"I hate to interrupt this lovely romance, but I must."

It was PeeWee, with the Warriors at his back.

"Hey, brothers," Gabriel said. If he was surprised he didn't let on. "You guys should have come earlier and taken the tour."

PeeWee smiled, but not in a friendly way. "We're here now, Mr. Liberator. Surely you can shake yourself free long enough to show us what's what."

Gabriel looked at the men, considering. "All right. If Mrs. Whittier doesn't mind, that is."

"No. No, go right ahead. I'll just continue with what I was doing," Rose said. The men, especially the little brazen one, gave her a bad feeling. She looked around. No one left looked like security. She sent Polly to sit with Roderick, who reposed in a corner with his nose in a book. Sitting in a chair in the adjacent kitchen, she breathed a silent prayer as she watched Gabriel head upstairs with the men.

She was still praying when he returned.

"We'll have Ping-Pong tables on the first floor," he was saying. "Plus a woodshop and a reading room. And we've secured a dental clinic on the upper level. Reverend Washington has some friends at the Midwestern State dental school."

PeeWee sneered. "Midwestern State? Where the white man teaches his lies? I thought this was about black youth! Better get some black dental students up in here."

"In case you didn't know, Howard U's in D.C.," Gabriel said. "That would be one hell of a commute."

One of the Warriors started to laugh, but PeeWee turned and stared at him with such intensity that he promptly swallowed his amusement.

"Unless you're talking about Meharry, but that's a far piece too," Gabriel continued. "I guess Midwestern is the best we can do."

"That's bullshit," PeeWee said vehemently. Across the gym, Polly and Roderick looked up. The band stopped playing.

PeeWee was undeterred. "Do we really want the white man coming in here and experimenting on our heads? On our children's heads?"

"You're getting loud, young man. It ain't that kind of party."

Without making a sound, Guts Tolliver had materialized in their midst. He eyed PeeWee with mild interest. The boy was all bluster, anyone could see that.

PeeWee turned to Guts. He stood barely higher than his belt. "We ain't got no beef with you, Big Man."

"You sure about that? Reverend Washington asked me to hang around and make sure everything's in order."

" 'Order' is a bourgeois tool of the oppressor," PeeWee said proudly. " 'Order' is the opiate of the masses."

Guts could tell that the young fellow was getting worked

up. Clearly he'd been imbibing something stronger than Vess cola.

"Come on, brother," Gabriel said, his arms outstretched. "We're all on the same side here."

PeeWee snickered. "Is that right, *brother*? Because we all haven't been going to the same meetings, have we? Some on our side don't even answer their phones anymore."

Guts had heard enough. "I'm sorry, you said your name was Little Pee, right? It ain't that kind of party, Little Pee. Come back when you got some hair on your chest."

Gateway's deadliest assassin looked at the Warriors. Eight strong, but pitifully weak without Gabriel to do their thinking. Aside from PeeWee, they were of various bulks and dimensions. A couple looked like they might have played high school football. Eight against one and Guts figured the odds were still in his favor.

"What say, fellas? Best catch some air, huh?"

The Warriors of Freedom looked at Guts, weighed their options, and decided that departing all in one piece was a damn fine idea.

PeeWee strutted close to Guts, his jaw jutting defiantly. "You don't scare me, Big Man," he said.

Guts thrust his head toward PeeWee faster than thought. "Boo!" he said.

PeeWee fainted, and the Warriors dragged him out.

Later that night, Guts gave the place a final go-round before heading home to bed. He nodded at two figures still in the parking lot and gave them a friendly wave. He recognized them as men of the Black Swan and knew they meant no harm. The reverend had said something about the men

painting a mural on the club's exterior with the help of neighborhood kids. Guts figured they were scoping the wall and
making plans.

Guts wheeled his sedan down Dodier Ave. toward Vandeventer, leaving Bob Cobb to sit patiently on the bumper of his
battered pickup, waiting for Talk Much to listen to his hands.
The tall, laconic sign painter pressed his palms against the corner of the boys' club and stood still with his eyes closed. Finally,
he opened his eyes and shook his head.

"Anything?" Bob Cobb asked.

"Nope," Talk Much said. "Too soon to tell."

Day Work

As casually as he could, Ed strolled through the South Side with his jacket draped over his shoulder. His tie, the same clip-on bow he wore to work, hung tentatively on his loosened collar. It had been part of his ruse. His parents believed he was heading straight to his job after school, but in reality he had left early with the approval of his guidance counselor. He hoped his dad didn't decide to stop at the store for a six-pack of Stag on his way home from the Black Swan.

Every street Ed crossed was unfamiliar, but he knew he couldn't go wrong if he stuck close to Kingshighway. That wide, busy boulevard stretched reassuringly for endless miles, all the way to the friendlier surroundings of North Gateway. Not that the South Side had been unfriendly. Despite the stories he'd heard about the tough whites of Dutchtown, Dago Hill, and other ethnic neighborhoods, no one had threatened his life so far.

He breathed easy despite seeing a police cruiser idling at a red light up ahead. He hadn't yet considered that the officers inside had been waiting for him.

"You're a bit far south, aren't you?"

The policeman on the driver's side wore aviator sunglasses. His elbow rested easily on the edge of his lowered window.

"A lot far south, I'd say," his partner added.

Ed put his hand to his brow to shield his eyes from the glare, but he still could not make out the partner's features.

"Yes, sir," Ed said, pleased that he'd remembered to say "sir." He went on to explain that he was returning from an interview.

"Don't imagine you'll get hired around here," the driver said, "but I guess they figured they had to talk to you."

He told Ed he might be more comfortable farther north, especially if he made it there before nightfall. Careful to look at each man and bow deferentially, Ed thanked the cops for their concern.

"Thank you, Officer, and thank you, sir. Well, so long."

The cops said nothing in reply. The driver simply grinned at Ed as he eased off the brake.

"So long." He'd gotten that from *The Andy Griffith Show*. Who could be sure that real-life white people said such things? He'd said it in a nasal, high-pitched voice. Similarly, he had tried his best to walk like a white boy, as if bouncing cheerfully along would make these strangers see Opie Taylor instead of his nervous black self, sweat glistening on his nose and upper lip.

It was Charlotte's fault. When he'd finally let on that he hadn't applied to Harvard after all, his pushy girlfriend had mentioned it to her boss. Apparently, Dr. Artinces Noel had connections. She made some calls, and suddenly he had a private interview with an important alum, an attorney with an office in South Gateway.

"Deliveries in the back," his secretary had said when, after changing buses twice, Ed finally found the law office nestled in a small professional building off the main drag.

Ed said nothing and gave her the chance to take in his jacket, tie, and businesslike manner. But she wasn't even looking at him. She resumed her filing and typing and seemed genuinely startled to turn around and find him still standing there.

When at last he gained an audience with the lawyer, a thoughtful, soft-spoken man in his late fifties, Ed found he had no trouble explaining himself. The lawyer nodded sympathetically at the appropriate parts and, when Ed finished, seemed kindly disposed.

"Harvard can do great things for you," he said. "But you could do at least as much for Harvard. With your background, your grades, and your work ethic, you'll make those prep-school boys look like the lazy, pampered dolts they are. My dad washed bottles at a brewery," he added with a wink.

"It's not too late for the fall," he said. "I have access to the admissions committee. Let me know."

"I have access," he'd said. Was access what the Warriors of Freedom were talking about when they shouted "Power to the People"? Was that what Dr. Noel had? My mother can make calls too, Ed thought. Look what she did for Rose Whittier, the lady who used to live next door. But Pristine didn't call that access. She called it the Lord making a way.

Ed paused at another stoplight. To his left he found a shopping strip. It had a Red Goose shoe store and a cake shop sandwiched between a Ben Franklin five-and-dime and a SuperMart. A kiosk on the parking lot sold keys and popcorn.

He looked at the SuperMart. It appeared to be much grander than the one he was used to. Curious to see how the other half worked, he headed for the entrance.

It was chilly inside, and not just from the air-conditioning. Ed was amazed to see how much bigger, brighter, and cleaner the store looked. Oblivious to the hostile stares of shoppers and employees alike, he gaped wonderingly at the fresher produce. There were more varieties of apples on display than he was aware existed. He passed by the Frosty-O's, the Hershey's Great Shakes, and the Pevely milk chilling in heavy glass bottles, suddenly intent on picking up a big bottle of Tahitian Treat to share with Crispus.

After locating it next to the Vess Orange Whistle, he grabbed a twenty-four-ounce bottle. He straightened up, and the manager tapped him on the shoulder.

"Need some help." He was a tall, fat man with long sideburns and a bad complexion. He didn't phrase it like a question.

"Not really, thanks. I'm just buying some soda and checking out the store."

"Checking it out for what?"

"I work for SuperMart too, on Natural Bridge."

The manager grunted and dug in his ear with a No. 2 pencil. With his other hand he tapped a clipboard impatiently against his thigh.

"North Side, huh?"

"Yep."

"Didn't even know they had groceries way up there, let alone SuperMarts."

Ed nodded. "Yeah, we have stores. Of course, with all the grass huts and wildlife, it's hard to make them out sometimes."

The manager squinted and began to drum the clipboard against his knee. "It's almost seven," he said. "Don't you want to be on your way."

These South Siders are so considerate, Ed thought. They all want me to get home before dark, and so anxious about it that they forget their question marks.

Outside the store with the Tahitian Treat safely in hand, Ed crossed the street and boarded the first of his three buses home.

The envelope was addressed to Rose Reynolds, and no one had called her that in years. That was the first thing that disturbed her. The return address said Joanne Whittier, and that was the second thing. Who could that be? Rose racked her brain, ran through a mental list of every one of Paul's female relatives whom she had ever met or heard about. She came up empty.

So she put the envelope on her dresser and busied herself with other things. At the end of the workday, she returned to Mrs. Garnett's and discovered, to her misery, that she hadn't imagined the envelope after all. She picked it up, sat on the edge of the bed, and took a deep breath. "My strength and my redeemer," she muttered. "Get ahold of yourself, girl."

Minutes later, the screen door on the front of the Garnett residence swung open with a bang. Mrs. Garnett, enjoying the comfort of a porch swing with Lucius Monday, turned to find Rose standing on the porch. She had her hands on her hips and a faraway look in her eyes.

"Everything okay, child?" Mrs. Garnett asked. She was genuinely concerned but having great difficulty turning away from Lucius for even a single minute.

"Fine," Rose said, not looking at either one of them. "I'll be back. Maybe."

"But where?—"

Rose was already down the steps and heading toward the corner. Mrs. Garnett stood up and followed her with her eyes. "I do declare," she exclaimed. "That child's not walking. She's *running.*"

On the bus, Ed took note of the half dozen or so black ladies carrying large shopping bags. The bags held the clothes they were required to wear when cleaning white people's houses. As soon as they got off work, they couldn't wait to put on outfits that better suited their real selves. So, though their feet were sore and their backs were tired, they sat upright in their dignified dresses, hats atop their heads like crowns.

Ed recognized his grandmother in their careworn faces. Reuben's mom, Nana, had spent a lifetime doing "day work," as it was politely called, until crippling arthritis forced her into a painful retirement.

Ed's reverie was interrupted by the bus driver. "Hellsfire!" he shouted from behind the wheel.

In the distance, a row of police cruisers stretched end to end, sirens flashing. A solitary policeman, standing in the path of the bus, waved it to the curb. The driver pulled over and the cop got on.

"Mayor's orders," the cop barked. "I'm shutting you down."

The driver was incredulous. "Shutting me down? What ever for?"

"Urban unrest," the cop said with a flourish. "No buses north of Manchester for the foreseeable future. Everybody off, please."

One of the day workers raised her hand. The cop pointed at her patiently, like a kindergarten teacher.

"How will we get home?"

"Best of luck, ma'am," the cop replied. "Tonight you're on your own."

Ed and the others got off and stood by the side of the road. At the gas station on the corner, a jackleg work crew was attaching plywood to the windows. Shirtless and lean, the workers were so tan and muscled that they looked like black men. Ed approached them and discovered they were not.

But they weren't unfriendly, just busy. As they hurried about their work, a few other stragglers from the bus joined Ed on the station's lot.

"Hurricane coming?" an old woman asked.

One of the workers, a cigarette hanging from his lips, turned and answered her. His tone was surprisingly polite. "Might could be, ma'am," he said. "Somethin' like that."

Ed and the others stared at the man. He took a long drag off his cigarette, pinched it and tossed it aside. "Y'all haven't heard, have you?"

Ed shook his head. "Heard what?"

"Some damn fool killed Martin Luther King," he said. "Shot him down dead in Memphis."

Ed gasped, the wind sucked from his body. One woman began to sob quietly. Another commenced to crying, high-pitched and keening. Yet another sat down quickly, as if punched by an invisible assailant. "Lord Jesus," she said.

*G*abriel was turning on the radio in his room when Rose burst in.

"Where's the fire?"

Rose grabbed his radio and yanked it from the wall. She leaped on Gabriel and knocked him flat on his back. Before he could speak or protest, she covered his mouth with hers.

*D*on't panic, Ed told himself. Kingshighway is a straight shot to the North Side. If folks go wild, and I suspect they will, I'll be watching them from the comfort of my third-floor window.

Two blocks up, he ran into another barricade. Police were steering all travelers, including pedestrians, away from a multiblock area containing Midwestern State and its hospital complex—the city's crown jewels. The detour would take him several miles out of his way. That's okay, he told himself, as long as I'm heading northeast. Toward home.

"*I*'m still a little confused here," Gabriel said. He and Rose had climbed from the floor to his bed. He couldn't believe it, Rose was finally in his bed. Fully clothed, but hey, that was a relatively minor obstacle.

"What?" Rose said. "But you swore to me that you could read."

"Very funny."

"Joanne Whittier is Paul's wife—a wife he never told me about. She's been trying to find me because she wants to divorce him. She's heard about me and wanted to warn me that Paul is liable to vanish without warning—just imagine that. To make a long story short, because Paul and Joanne never divorced, Paul and I were never married."

Gabriel couldn't help smiling. "So I've got a single woman up in here?"

"That's right."

Gabriel looked at Rose like he was three seconds from tearing her clothes off. Maybe two seconds . . .

"A single woman but a godly one," Rose said, sitting up suddenly. Coming back to her senses, she realized that the wild-eyed woman who'd run all the way to the rectory and *jumped* on poor Gabriel Patterson was actually *her*.

"Okay," Gabriel said.

Then he and Rose were at it again, kissing furiously. They stopped, breathing hard. "We gotta find the reverend," Gabriel said.

They stood up, and once again Rose straightened her clothes.

There was a knock at the door. Gabriel looked at Rose. She shrugged.

The second series of knocks was more insistent. Gabriel opened the door, and PeeWee Jefferson came flying in.

He dispensed with the pleasantries and began shouting immediately. "Brother man, it's on!"

"What's on?"

"You don't know? What have y'all been doin'?"

PeeWee slowed down for the first time since entering. His eyes shifted back and forth from Gabriel to Rose. "No time for none of that tonight," he said. "Sorry about that, but warriors have no choice. Isn't that right, Gabriel? Mr. Liberator? You used to say that all the time. Warriors have no choice."

"I still don't get why you're here," Gabriel said. "Has something happened?"

"Turn on the radio, brother. King is dead."

"Oh, no," Rose said. She sank to the bed, deflated.

"Oh, yeah," PeeWee corrected. "The Peacemaker got shot down, and now warriors can rise up." He turned and spoke softly to Gabriel, who remained frozen in one spot.

"I got the brothers together and they got the goods. We can *move* on some shit tonight."

"I won't be moving with you."

PeeWee got in Gabriel's face. "I know I'm not hearing you right."

Gabriel backed away, hands up. "Leave it, PeeWee. I got other priorities now."

PeeWee jerked a thumb in Rose's direction. "Women? Is that what you're talking about?"

Gabriel smiled at Rose. "Marriage, actually. Marriage is what I'm talking about."

"My man," PeeWee said. He was struggling to be patient. "Marriage is the opiate of the masses."

"Said the man who's never even been with a woman," Rose said, dripping contempt.

PeeWee turned on her, eyes blazing. "Bitch, I'll—"

Gabriel moved swiftly, throwing the smaller man to the floor. He sank a knee into PeeWee's chest and drew back his fist.

"No! No, Gabriel. Don't be that kind of man. Please."

Rose's pleading calmed Gabriel. He removed his knee from PeeWee's chest. He stood up, took a step back, and looked sadly at his former friend.

"This is how it starts," he said.

PeeWee scrambled to his feet, whipped a handgun from his waistband, and pressed the snout to Gabriel's forehead. "Nigger," he said, "I should shoot you where you stand."

Neither man moved or spoke. The only sound was breathing and Rose's fiercely uttered prayers. At last PeeWee pulled the gun away and stuffed it behind his back. Staring at Gabriel, he backed slowly toward the door.

" 'Nigger'? What happened to 'Brother'?"

Ignoring him, PeeWee slipped away as quickly as he had come.

Rose collapsed in Gabriel's arms, sobbing.

"Just when I finally have you, I almost lose you," she said.

"It will be just fine, baby," Gabriel said, rubbing her back. "You and me together. Just fine."

Burning Desires

*t*he backseat of Ananias Goode's New Yorker was surprisingly roomy. Of course, the extra space might have been attributable to unusual factors: (1) Mr. Goode was not in the car, and (2) Rose Whittier—make that Reynolds—was sitting on Gabriel's lap. Guts Tolliver rolled smoothly through North Gateway's burning streets while Rev. Washington joined together what no man should tear asunder.

"I now pronounce you man and wife," he said, as the midnight blue sedan crossed Delmar Boulevard. If he'd been looking out the window instead of at his Bible, he might have spotted Pristine Jones's eldest son making his way up Vandeventer.

"I can't thank you enough," Gabriel said.

"Don't mention it, and don't forget to thank Mr. Goode, who was kind enough to lend us his car, and Mr. Tolliver, who was kind enough to donate his services as well."

Guts looked in the rearview mirror and tipped his hat.

They rode in comfortable serenity as the car rolled into the city's fashionable West End. Under an immense baronial arch, a policeman granted them entry to a gated community where lush splendor muffled all outside noise. Inside Parkmoor, the riots might as well have been a rumor.

The car eased to a stop beside an immense, beautiful mansion. "To consummate your union," Rev. Washington said to the astonished pair. He held before them a key on a length of jeweled chain.

"You'll find everything you need inside, once again courtesy of Ananias Goode. He asks your forgiveness, he says, but it was the best he could do under such urgent circumstances."

The New Yorker eased away. Gabriel leaned forward and placed the key in the lock. Before he could turn it, Rose grabbed his wrist.

"Gabriel."

"What is it?"

"Is this crazy?"

"Crazy? What do you mean?"

"Reverend King is dead. Years from now, our children will ask us about this night. How we reacted. What we did."

Gabriel smiled and kissed Rose on the nose. "We'll tell them that while everyone around us was losing their minds, we did the one thing that made sense."

A spotlight, bigger than a console television, came whistling out of the sky. It crashed to earth a few yards behind Ed, sending glass and metal shrapnel in several directions. Ed caught only a few shards in his back and shoulders. Ahead of him, fire and smoke billowed from burned out stores, piles of tires, garbage—anything that could sustain a flame. Sooty and wild-eyed, North Siders pushed pilfered shopping carts full of other people's stuff. Beauty supplies, groceries, blackboard erasers, car parts—they all rolled by. Other people, mostly youngsters, simply wreaked havoc, happily tossing firebombs and throwing rocks. The spotlight had come from a billboard mounted on a roof three stories up. Parched and exhausted as he neared Royal Packing Company, Ed saw two slender, barefoot women carrying a huge couch. They lugged it as easily as utility workers handling a telephone pole.

$\mathcal{O}$n Sullivan Avenue, some streetlights were working perfectly. Others sputtered in and out, creating a strobelike effect. Reuben and Pristine huddled with Shom and Crisp beside the radio. Pristine's station was playing snippets of King's speeches between gospel songs and commentary. The couple only half-listened to the broadcast, unable to pay full attention to anything until Ed arrived. SuperMart closed at nine.

Mr. Collins rapped on the door and asked Reuben to step onto the porch. Pristine, by now familiar with that gambit, stepped out also.

The light in front of the house sputtered violently, then left them in blackness. Mr. Collins's voice was suddenly disembodied. "The store's burning," he said. "They think they have everybody out, but—"

"What store?" Pristine asked, but for Reuben realization had already dawned. Fishing his car keys out of his pocket, he leaped off the porch.

"Stay away from Vandeventer," Mr. Collins called after him. "It's not moving at all."

But Reuben didn't hear him. He'd already started the car.

Pristine was silent, but Mr. Collins was certain she was crying. "I'm sorry," he said.

"I know."

"I've got to get back to Dessie."

"Of course."

Pristine, cheeks glistening, heard him leave the porch and

cut across the lawn. She opened the door and went back inside to her boys.

Just beyond Royal Packing Company, across Easton Avenue, two paddy wagons and a commandeered travel bus lined the curb. As soon as Ed set foot on Easton, he found himself being violently herded toward the waiting vehicles. A phalanx of policemen had formed behind the group, a shoulder-to-shoulder wall of Plexiglas and impatience. Jostled and prodded and rushed, Ed moved double-time to avoid being trampled. Even so he caught an elbow in the mouth and a sharp knee in his upper thigh. He'd lost his jacket, and his shirt, once crisply white, was now tattered and stained. The Tahitian Treat fell beneath the mob. His bow tie, improbably, hung on.

$\mathcal{R}$euben's Rambler turned the corner on two wheels. Two blocks later, it skidded to a halt. Traffic was bumper to bumper and no one was moving. He got out of the car. To his right, the plate-glass window of Hammers Cleaners had a car-size hole in it. A few people gathered on the sidewalk and waited nervously while someone inside handed pants, dresses, coats, and hats through the opening.

The fire hydrants from the corner to Fairgrounds Park had all been set loose, flooding Vandeventer. Here and there, people splashed between the cars.

"They got Natural Bridge locked down," Reuben heard someone shout. "Ain't no cars gettin' through." Reuben cursed. He locked the car—lotta good that's going to do, he briefly thought—and set off on foot past Burk's Funeral Parlor on Ashland Avenue. He came out at Warne Avenue two blocks later and turned left on Natural Bridge.

Back on Sullivan, Mrs. Cleveland had just sucked down a soda and sauntered out into the middle of the street. In the shadowy half-light she appeared to be leaning on a stick. She was quickly joined by Mrs. Scott, the kindly old neighbor whom everyone called Aunt Georgia. Watching from the window with Shom and Crispin, Pristine saw the women commiserating beneath a fluttering streetlight.

Pristine turned away, missing the young thug who appeared beside the two old women. Holding his crotch and spitting, he spoke in a threatening voice.

"What y'all ladies got to share? Hmm, what you bitches got?"

Aunt Georgia sighed and squinted at the boy. She said, "The Lord loves a cheerful giver, but I guess I'm just not in the mood."

The thug moved his hand from his crotch to his scalp, still scratching. "What the hell's that supposed to mean?"

Mrs. Cleveland raised and pumped her walking stick, which, it turned out, was a double-barreled shotgun.

"It means take one more step," she said, "and I'll blast you to hell, you ignorant-ass bastard."

*O*ut of breath, with sharp, mysterious pains in his mouth and upper thigh, Reuben arrived at the intersection of Fair Avenue and Natural Bridge. From there he could see that part of the SuperMart was still standing. He got closer and saw that most of it had been reduced to smoldering rubble. The air was thick with the funk of burning meat, scorched milk, and the dusty remnants of sugar, flour, and assorted grains. Bottles and cans of chemicals—oven cleaners and hair sprays—

alternately popped and crumpled in the heat. Here and there, rough edges of brick still glowed with the orange light of living flames.

The parking lot looked like the triage unit of an emergency ward. Bits of words rode the hot winds like ashes and embers. Flakes of language—"collapsed lungs," "burned beyond recognition"—tortured Reuben's ears. He approached the least wounded, those reclining on the ground, propped up on elbows or sitting calmly beside the ambulances and fire trucks.

"Have you seen Ed? I'm Ed's dad. Have you seen him? Ed Jones?"

The shock was deeper than it seemed. Ed's co-workers were somber, uncommunicative, unable to meet Reuben's eyes. He felt his temper getting the best of him.

Helpless and bellowing, he tore through the yellow crime scene tape, headed straight for the smoky wreck of the Super-Mart. Two cops collared him before he got very far.

"Back off, buddy," one warned. He turned to his partner. "Fucking looters," he said.

"It's my son," Reuben yelled. "It's my son! It's my son! It's my son!"

The larger cop yanked Reuben's arm behind his back and twisted it upward. His partner thrust his baton—hard—into Reuben's sternum. At best it would leave a bruise. At worst he'd cracked a rib.

"You crazy fucks wanna burn yourselves up, go right ahead," the short cop said. "But do it somewhere else. Don't let me see your ass around here any more tonight."

He withdrew his baton. The big cop released Reuben's arm and shoved him to the ground.

Dazed and delirious, Reuben staggered home through a

world he no longer recognized. Along Vandeventer, the street-lights blew out one by one, like birthday candles.

*H*andcuffed, sitting haunch to haunch in an over-stuffed bus full of young, sweaty, violent, angry colored men, Ed found himself recalling Rev. Miles Washington's many sermons about the fiery pits of hell. Trapped amid the pandemonium, he gave up on the possibility of hearing his own thoughts. He wondered if he'd even retain the ability to hear anything at all.

The police had turned the interior lights all the way on, coating everything and everyone in a sick, mustardy glare.

"What they gon' do next, gas us?"

"Nigger go out for chitlins, look where he end up."

"This shit's illegal. Don't let my black ass get hold of a lawyer."

"Damn, ain't they got bathwater at your house?"

"Bet we make some noise, they'll let us out."

A chant rose up: "Let us out! Let us out! Let us out!"

The bus began to rock from side to side.

Ed closed his eyes and slumped back in his tiny patch of seat.

*P*ristine and the two younger boys met Reuben at the door. He had been gone roughly an hour. Limping, dirty, wet, sooty, and bruised, he looked like a soldier returning from a long and brutal war.

They sent the boys to their room. She helped Reuben to the kitchen and guided him into a chair. She slid his shirt gingerly from his limbs. She ran warm water in the sink and sponged his sore chest. The house was silent except for the gentle drone of the radio.

She hadn't asked her husband a single question. When he was ready, he would talk.

"Not much of the building left," he finally said. "Every-body's not accounted for. Some folks . . . some folks . . . they couldn't recognize."

Pristine held Reuben to her chest. He sobbed like a drown-ing man hungry for air, desperately, without sound. He calmed, and they clung together, immobile, until the sound of tinkling glass opened their eyes. They found Crispus pouring red soda—Tahitian Treat—into a glass.

He looked at his parents. "Ed will be thirsty when he comes," he told them.

"*L*et us out! Let us out!"

The noise abruptly ended when the bus doors opened with a hiss. Ed looked up to see a black detective step onboard, accompanied by two uniformed officers. The voices on the bus, so raucous before, remained respectfully subdued.

"That's Grimes," someone whispered. "That black-glove-wearin' muthafucka is crazy to the bone."

Grimes strolled all the way to the back of the bus, then reversed himself, causing the two uniforms to stumble and col-lide. They quickly righted themselves and waited to see what he would do next. Grimes turned his head neither left nor right, but no one doubted he would find the one he came for.

Ed was completely surprised when Grimes stopped before his seat, lifted his chin with his gloved hand, and looked him in the eyes. He nodded to the uniforms. They moved forward and unlocked Ed's cuffs.

"Come with us," one of them said.

In the detective's car, Ed shook the feeling back into his wrists. "I remember you," he said. "You came to the Black Swan."

Grimes drove in silence.

"Where are you taking me?"

"Home."

Ed brightened. "For real? Why?"

"I owe your father."

Ed couldn't help grinning. He clapped his hands and laughed out loud. "You mean my old man has access? Damn."

Tahitian Treat

*O*ur parents had allowed us downstairs again. They sat silently in the kitchen, waiting for bad news to come in and make itself at home. Mom had wrapped Dad's chest in a broad white bandage and helped him put on a clean shirt. He slumped a bit in his chair and stared out into space. In the background, Rev. Josiah Banks was talking about dreams and mountaintops. I wondered when the minister found time to sleep.

The television in the living room was on, but the volume was turned down. Neither Shom nor I complained as a succession of talking heads told the nation how to feel.

I stood up.

"Where you going?" Shom demanded.

"To the third floor."

"Like hell," Shom said. "You're too scared to go up there. You ain't nothin' but a pun——"

"Shut up or I'll call the zombies," I blurted.

Shom stared, shocked.

"That's right, you heard me. I'll tell them where you live. On a night like this, who could stop them? Who would even notice? Anything else?"

Ashen, Shom shook his head.

"I didn't think so," I said, and I turned for the stairs. I had no time to savor my rare triumph. I needed to get Ed home. I entered his room in the dark, trying not to look at the grotesque skull glowing on the wall.

I went over to the bureau. I knew Ed hadn't thrown away his Murray's and his stocking cap, even though he told everybody that he had. He'd stuffed them in the corner of his bottom drawer while telling me exactly why Marvel was so superior to DC. I fished around and got them out. I headed for the door, then changed my mind.

Stocking cap and pomade in hand, I stood in front of the skull. If you looked at it long enough and from the right angle, its greedy, gaping mouth turned into a friendly smile, like Casper's.

"That's right," I told the skull. "Sir Crispus the Pure-Hearted rides again."

Downstairs, I stood in front of the mirror for longer than I'd ever dared. I rubbed a dollop of Murray's between my palms like I'd watched Ed do a million times. I slathered it into my hair, smoothed it carefully with my hands, and put on the stocking cap.

I walked downstairs and sat in front of the Tahitian Treat I'd poured. It was going to need some ice. Without turning, I could feel my family staring at my new look. "It reminds me of Ed," I said.

The light was slowly returning to my dad's eyes. He reached out to pat my shoulder and tell me that he understood when something else caught his attention. I turned and saw it too, through the living room window: flashing lights in front of the house.

My parents rose, gripped hands, and headed for the door. My dad groaned—an awful, horrible sound, like an animal trapped at the bottom of a well—and my mother prayed. Loudly. Swiftly. Furiously.

The doorbell rang. My mother opened the door and screamed. A black policeman, a detective, was standing on our porch. In front of him stood Reuben Edward Jones Jr., home at last.

We all hugged Ed, making him ache even more than he already did. But he didn't seem to mind. Between his blubbering and our blubbering, bits of information filtered through. We said stuff like love, missed, and happy. He said stuff like Harvard, interview, and access.

"Dad has access," he kept saying.

It would, we agreed, make better sense in the light of day.

While we babbled, Dad walked the policeman to his car. Later he told us he had asked Detective Grimes why he rescued Ed.

"You gave me my daughter back," he replied. "I owed you one."

We settled in the kitchen. Mom began to stir up something tasty while we sipped Tahitian Treat.

"The King of Love is dead," said a voice on the radio.

My mother crossed the room and switched it off. "Reverend King has passed on," she said. "But love? Love's not going anywhere."

Stretching her slender arm, she passed her hand above the heads of all her sons. She ruffled Ed's growing wool. She teased Shom's soft curls. She tickled my beanshots, stocking cap and all. Releasing a small, defiant yelp of joy, she sat on my father's lap and pressed her nose to his. Then she pulled back to look into the eyes she'd loved since she was a teenager in bobby socks.

"God is good," she said. Then she kissed Dad on the mouth.